PANDORA

by Holly Hollander

PANDORA
by Holly Hollander

a novel by

GENE WOLFE

A Tom Doherty Associates Book
NEW YORK

PANDORA BY HOLLY HOLLANDER

Copyright © 1990 by Gene Wolfe

A Tor Book
Published by Tom Doherty Associates, Inc.
49 West 24th Street
New York, N.Y. 10010

ISBN: 0-312-85010-7

Printed in the United States of America

First edition: December 1990

0 9 8 7 6 5 4 3 2 1

To Aladdin Blue and David G. Hartwell,
because this is mostly their fault.

FOREWORD

Is this a historical novel?, you ask. Nope. This is just one that took a real long time to sell. (Except in France, so *vive la France!* It almost makes me wish I'd taken French instead of Latin.)

It's also the *only* book of mine to sell, so far. I started writing it the day after I moved in with Blue, but it took over a year to get it finished and it hung around various publishers' offices for about as long as it would've taken me to get through college, assuming I'd gone to college.

Then Ms. Sudden down at the BPL introduced me to this real writer who knows Joe Hensley and everything. We got to talking, and it turned out that I'd had three or four classes with his daughter. So he wrote it all over again putting in a lot more commas, and they say they're going to run his name on the title page with mine. Only Hartwell wanted more about Larry Lief, so now we've put that in, too.

Altogether it's been one hell of a time, but Barton hasn't changed a lot. (Here I'm awfully tempted to tell you all about how I met Abbie Hoffman, and the first time I smoked dope, and the last time, and bunches of other stuff. But that's all after the end, so why should you care?) The Ben Franklin Store's been squeezed out by more boutiques. Some new people own the Magic Key now, and they don't call it that. The worst thing by a long shot is that Uncle De Witte Sinclair's dead. I could tell you quite a bit about that; but you wouldn't want to read it. And to tell you the truth, I wouldn't want to write it. So long, Uncle Dee. Kisses.

Holly H. Hollander
Barton, Illinois
1990

1

How the Box Got to Barton

THE *German 88 mm. gun was undoubtedly the most fa-mous artillery piece of World War II. It fired a 22 lb. shell and could pick off a tank a mile away. The Germans called it the "Gun Flak"; it weighed 5.5 tons, it had an extreme range of nine miles, and it killed thousands of Russian, British, and American soldiers.*

I got all that out of a book.

A shell from a German 88 almost killed my father, twice. I didn't get that from the book—he told me about the first time.

My father is George Henry Hollander. In his company, which is Hollander Safe & Lock, they call him G. H. Hollander. Anyhow I guess they do, because he took me down to their headquarters one time—they rent four floors of this big building in the Loop—and that was what it said on his door: "G. H. Hollander, Chief Operating Officer." Only his business cards say: "G. H. 'Harry' Hollander." I used to have one of those cards around here, but I guess I lost it.

Anyway, he lied about how old he was and joined the

army in 1943, when he was seventeen. He said he figured he never would get drafted, because his father was Herbert Hollander and had so much money, and he was going to this private school in the east, and he hated it. So one night he hitchhiked into New York, and spent the rest of the night walking around and sitting in bars and what he calls one-arm joints. And the next day he told them he was eighteen and hadn't registered for the draft, but now he wanted to enlist. He trained in America for a couple of months, I guess, and then they sent him overseas, and he was in one of the waves that landed at Anzio. I forget which wave, but not the first. Anyway, he was a supply clerk in an infantry company, and later on he was the supply sergeant. The day that he landed, this 88 shell smacked into the sand right at his feet. He said he heard it coming, only he hadn't learned to flop down without thinking, the way he did later. If it had gone off, it would've killed him for sure, and I wouldn't be here writing this.

The second time is kind of funny, because he wasn't even there. But before I tell you about it, I think I ought to tell you a little about me and my father and mother and Barton, and Barton Hills, which is where we were all living then.

My name's Holly H. Hollander. The *H* is for Henrietta, so you can see why I don't use it. My mother—her name's Elaine Calvat (that's pronounced Kal-VAH)—wanted a cute name, and I was born on Christmas Eve. My father wanted me named for him, because it must have been awfully obvious even back then that there weren't going to be any more kids. I'm older now than my father was when he joined the army, which really wipes me out.

If you've been adding and subtracting, you will have seen that my father was pretty well up there already when I was born, but my mother was only about twenty-three. She used to be his secretary, and she's quite a bit younger than he is.

Maybe you want to know what we look like. You've seen guys like my father around quite a bit, I guess, if you're the kind of person who serves on boards of directors. He's big. He has short gray hair and one of those old noble-Roman faces. He used to be on the stout side, if you know what I mean, but since all this happened he's lost some weight and looks a little younger. I remember one time a couple of years ago when he had a bunch of men like him out to the house. I always shake hands with guys, because I can tell they like it, and afterward I went over and felt my father's hands because the ones I had been shaking felt so yucky. His were the only ones that weren't soft. He used to say that if things had been different he would've made somebody a good mechanic, and I think he was right. He had a shop in our basement with a lot of tools, and at night sometimes he worked on some of the stuff the company made, and lots of other things.

My mother's a natural blonde, with that straight hair that looks like it's been ironed. Us Hollanders are supposed to be Dutch if you go back far enough, and the Calvats are supposed to be French; but Elaine's the one with the blond hair and the kind of skin you think you can see through. Only I've always thought of Dutch girls as having these round, apple cheeks, and Elaine's certainly aren't like that. She has this perfect almost heart-shaped little face you see sometimes on sexy girls in the comic strips—the kind that goes just super with a hat about the size of a cold-cream jar that cost five hundred dollars. To tell the truth, my mother never used to look like my mother; she looked like she was about thirty, which would make her my big sister, and quite a few times she asked me to pretend she was my aunt. Sometimes I used to think I was adopted. Nobody would ever say it was true, and I know that lots of kids think that— half of my friends at Barton High did—but for me it wasn't as crazy as it sounds.

I'm kind of tall, but not real tall. My hair's brown, like my father's was before it turned gray. It's curly, and I let it grow long enough to hang a good way down my back. I tan and I'm usually pretty brown, and I have strong arms; all that's because I really love tennis and horses—especially horses. We used to have a little stable, and I had an Arabian gelding called Sidi ben Sahid. We had a tennis court, too. Sidi's gone now, but I still hitch up to North Park two or three times a week to play on the courts there. There's room for a horse here, and someday I'm going to buy Sidi back, or anyway buy another horse, maybe a jumper.

Let's see, what else?

I swim quite a bit when it's warmer. I used to blast cans off the fence with my .22, and now I'm pretty good at squirrels. My eyes are brown, my face is squarer than Elaine's, with high cheekbones, and my nose turns up in a way that I guess makes me look snotty sometimes. I'm not very big up top, but the shape's good. I have this little waist that I can nearly get my hands around (which is something nobody seems to care about any more, although from Jane Austen and like that it seems to me it used to be terribly important), and good hips and legs. Kris, a guy I used to go with, said I had the greatest ankles in the world. Since I've already mentioned Jane Austen, maybe I ought to come right out and admit that I read quite a bit, even though that's a crime or something now, and you wouldn't think it to look at me. I wear contacts for reading, and for tennis and squirrel hunting, and sometimes for other stuff.

When I was a little kid in Middle School the teachers were always asking what we wanted to be when we grew up. Well, I'm grown up now, and I guess since you're reading this it's pretty obvious what one thing I want to be is. I want to be a writer. I also want to be an adventuress. (I'm as liberated as you are, but adventurer doesn't really mean the same thing, now does it?) I'm going to have a ton of adventures, and write about them when they're over—like this—and sleep with rock stars and then sue them.

Okay, now you know quite a bit about me, and my father and mother. Barton is a town of about 10,000 and it's 65 miles by car from the Loop. Lots of pretty wealthy people live in Barton, but the really rich ones live west of it in Barton Hills, where every house has to have at least twenty acres. The high school and fire department are both in Barton. (Barton Hills has its own police force, with maybe three cops and two cars.) I don't think there's a building in Barton that's more than two floors high, not counting the water tower.

From what I've told you already, you can guess that in and around Barton there are quite a lot of ladies who have quite a bit of money and quite a bit of spare time. Which means there are lots of social affairs of one kind and another; some of them make me laugh, but it isn't all bad. Like, they run a regular store, the Snatchpenny, where you can buy donated stuff—clothes that don't exactly fit somebody any more (or maybe never did), third toasters, and like that. I live in jeans and denim shirts mostly, and they never seem to get those, but even so I've found some real bargains, like my sheepskin coat for nineteen ninety-five this winter. The ladies clerk for free maybe half a day a week, and all the money goes to Barton Community Hospital. They put on plays, too, and dances, and there are clubs for handball and horseshoes and so forth, and *two* literary societies—one for people who want to talk about books that have been dramatized on TV and one for people who don't.

But the biggie, the really big, big deal, comes at the end of July. Most Barton families take their vacations in January or February and go to Bermuda or the Virgin Islands, because the winters can be really mean here but the summers are nice. But even if they didn't, I think that almost everybody would try to schedule things so they were in town for it. What it is, is the Barton Antique Fair and Art Festival. Usually we just call it the Fair. People bring antiques from as far as Philadelphia to show for prizes, and there's a couple of auctions, and a lot of stuff that's just for sale at a set price, like a thousand bucks for an early colonial banister-backed chair or maybe twenty-five for a 19th-century sauer-kraut crock. There's a used-book sale where the books go for anything from a hundred dollars to five-for-a-buck, and an art show, and an art auction, and a whole lot of artists who come to sell their work direct—sketches and oils and watercolors, and sculptures and woodcarvings and a lot of other junk. And there's always a special event that's different every year.

The Fair takes over all of Barton High and spills out into the grounds in front; and people park their cars in the parking lots, and all over all three softball diamonds, and all up and down Main Street. The really valuable antiques are inside the classrooms just in case it rains, although it hardly ever does. The art show is in the art rooms upstairs, and the book sale's upstairs in the chem lab. The artists set up outside if they're selling paperweights and that kind of junk, and inside if they have paintings and real reputations. There's a Gourmet French Lunch fixed in the kitchen. (Would you believe it's the Lions who do that? Most years they have quiche Lorraine, fresh French bread and butter, tossed salad, some kind of dessert crepe, and a choice of regular or decaf, tea, or milk. It costs $5.50 or so. My father used to be a Lion, and I helped serve once.) And outside there are burger stands and so on.

So that's the fill-in on *that*.

Last year's is the Fair I want to tell about. Like I said, my father was in the Lions and of course Elaine was big in the Women's Club, which is the basic outfit that puts on the fair. She had been secretary and treasurer and corresponding secretary and vice president twice and God knows what else, so eventually it got to be her turn to be the chairwoman of the fair. (That's why they call it: "chairwoman." I'd say *chair*, but then I'd never run an outfit like that anyway.) I guess most of it's pretty cut and dried. They have lists of people—artists and exhibitors—who have to be notified, and there are standing committees for the book sale and

6

parking and auctions and all that. The hard part was, you guessed it, the special event.

Like one year they had this mystery exhibition. There were all sorts of old kitchen gadgets and beauty aids and tools, and you had to write down what everything was called and what it was used for, and there were prizes. (One mystery item was a round iron weight with a handle on top, and I'll give you half of it, it was called a *frog*. Do you know what it was good for? I didn't think so.) Another year it was a hot-air balloon, with a long rope to hold it and the balloonist dressed up in real old circus style like the Great and Powerful Oz; and he'd take your kid up free if you could show a receipt that proved you'd bought something that cost more than fifty dollars.

Now it was my mother's turn, and you couldn't repeat. She had to come up with something good if she wanted to hold up her head afterward with the rest of the ex-chair-women, and I'm here to tell you she damn near went crazy. Elaine wasn't the easiest person in the whole world to live with even when everything was going right, and that was pure hell. My father used to say that Elaine never had an idea in her life, but there for a month or more—May and the first bit of June—she was having two or three a day, and most of them weren't worth doodly, just warmed-over things that had been done before and things that nobody but God could do (and maybe not even Him) and things that nobody'd care whether you did or not. A few were maybe halfway good, but she couldn't even see that. Finally it got so bad I started feeling sorry for her instead of just yelling back and locking myself in my room or going off for a ride on Sidi; she was my mother after all, and when she was at her absolute worst I could see that we were related after all even if she did have creamy big ones and that little heart-shaped face with that cute mouth. Because to tell you the truth I'm like that sometimes. In fact I'm like that a lot.

Anyway, one Saturday morning my father couldn't take

it any longer. It was only about nine o'clock, but he went and got his checkbook and wrote her a check and said, "Here, go shopping. I don't care how you spend it, but don't come back till the stores close." I didn't get to see how much it was, but it must have been a thousand at least, because when Elaine looked at it her mouth made a little O the way it does sometimes, and to Elaine anything under a grand was chicken feed. Then she ran upstairs to get dressed, and she told my father to call Bill and have him get his uniform on. Bill Hake was the man who took care of our cars and the garden, and helped me take care of Sidi.

So my father called Bill on the house phone and told him to get dressed up and bring around the Caddy, and he said, "Drive slowly, Bill, and if you should find yourself headed back here before dark, have engine trouble." Bill wasn't long on brains, but he could be kind of tricky. I've never seen a servant yet who couldn't, unless he was new; it seems like it's something they all learn.

Anyway Elaine came back about seven that night. My father and I were in his study, where he had his office stuff and his souvenirs and books; and maybe that was his tough luck. She was walking on air. "Wait till you see it! Wait till you see it!" That's all she'd say, and she kind of waltzed around the room for us. When she stopped, she got my face between her hands and kissed me. I think it was the first time she'd kissed me since I was a little kid.

Right then Bill came in. He was carrying a box about two feet long and maybe eighteen inches wide and a foot deep, and the sweat was standing out on his face like he was about to keel over. He said, "Where you want it, Mrs. Hollander?" Naturally Elaine said on the coffee table, which had a glass top. So Bill set it down in the middle of the floor and straightened up with both hands on the small of his back like he would never be the same. I said, "What's in it?" and bounced over to have a look.

As heavy as it seemed to be, I expected it to be solid iron, but it was wood—some kind of old, dark-reddish wood with brass corners and wide brass bands and a big, complicated-looking iron lock. It was old, you could see that right away; so old that it made me think about stagecoaches and those western flicks where the bad guys make the driver throw down the Wells Fargo box.

And on the lid, in that big fat curly gold-leaf lettering they used back then (you could still read it, although the gold was tarnished and a lot had been chipped away) it said PANDORA.

2

How I Met Aladdin Blue

IT was about two weeks after the Pandora box came that we heard about Uncle Herbert. Those places are very discreet, it seems, because I saw their letter, and to look at it you wouldn't have thought it came from a hospital or anything like one. I'd have said a classy resort hotel like the Greenbrier, maybe, except that the stationery was too subdued even for them. The paper was about the size of a page in a library book, good paper, not that ostentatious stuff that tries to look like vellum (I've never seen real vellum—has anybody?), and the lettering on it was pale blue and no bigger than the fine print on those forms that tell you everything the company won't do for you. There was a little pale blue pergola with chairs under it, and that was all. Very cool. It was called Garden Meadow; I had heard my father and Elaine talking about it. The way I got to see the letter was by sneaking into my father's study. He had taken his mail and gone in there, and about five minutes later he came out looking funny, so I thought, oh boy, something's up.

The fact is I'd done that sort of thing before, and I knew

the letter would be in his wastebasket or on his desk, because his secretary, Joan Robush, came out once a week to take care of the filing for him. You can call it being nosy if you want to, or you can call it caring about your family and what happens to them. Or you can call it being a detective. Those things all depend on how you look at them.

Anyway, it said: *Mr. Herbert Hollander III is presently experiencing some discomfort. Dr. Peabody has arranged for an overnight visit to St. Mary of the Lake, which has X-ray facilities; and while we feel there is no immediate cause for alarm, we wish to keep you informed.*

There was a lot more, naturally; but that was the part that counted. My parents were having a late breakfast on the patio, so I went out there—they got very quiet when they saw me coming—and sat down with them. After ten minutes or so Elaine left because she had an appointment with her hairdresser, and I asked my father if he was going to see his brother.

"How did you know?" he said, looking at me in that way that wilts vice presidents.

"I didn't know," I told him, "that's why I asked. I'd like to tag along."

"How did you know that Bert is sick?"

"The mail came, and I heard you talking to Elaine like something had happened."

"Well, you can't go," he said, and that was that. Pretty soon I heard the Mercedes purring down our private road, and I was left alone on the patio with the warm summer air, the cold coffee, and some muffins. (I prefer cupcakes.)

I don't think I ever even wondered whether I ought to go see my Uncle Herbert or not. Here was my father's brother only about fifty miles away, and I'd never met him, and now he was, most likely, getting set to die. I knew that Garden Meadow was a couple of miles north of a little country place called Dawn, which isn't really much farther from Chicago than Barton. And I wasn't really a kid any more, whether my father understood that or not. Sitting there on the chaise, thinking about everything and cussing, I decided that I was going to go anyhow, timing it so he'd be gone when I got there. They'd have to let me in—I was Herbert Hollander's niece, practically next of kin. All I'd have to do was tell them I'd had an appointment of some kind and couldn't come with my father, but I came as soon as I could.

The way I saw it there were three ways I could get there. The easy one would be to drive. I didn't have my license yet, but I'd taken Driver's Ed that year and the Ford wagon that Mrs. Maas, our housekeeper, used for shopping was in the garage. The problem with that was that I'd be in trouble even if my father didn't find out I'd gone to Garden Meadow. Mrs. Maas would be sure to tell him, and besides it would have meant waiting around to get the timing right, and I was in no mood to wait around.

The next easiest would be to call up somebody who'd drive me. Les and a couple more girlfriends had cars, and Kris would have given ten bucks to do it. The trouble with that was that it would get out for sure that I had a relative in the crack-up college. For myself I wouldn't have minded— I act pretty crazy half the time anyway—but I knew my father didn't want it talked around town and Elaine would throw a fit. Anyway, my big point was that I was grown up enough now to be trusted; and if I let somebody else in on our private stuff like that, I'd be proving right there that they were right and I was wrong.

That left the hardest way. But it wasn't really so hard, and I had plenty of time. The Chicago, Wisconsin & Northern runs commuter trains—every hour on the hour, after the morning rush—between Barton and Chicago. And it stood to reason that there'd have to be several Greyhounds a day going from Chicago to Dawn and, as they say, points west. So all I had to do was get to Barton to catch a train.

Riding Sidi would have meant leaving him tied up someplace for most of the day and maybe getting him stolen; I wasn't about to do that. Riding my bike would've made a lot more sense, but it would mean parking it at the railway station, a sure tip-off that I'd gone into Chicago to anybody that knew me. That left walking. It's a little over four miles; but I'd done it before, and besides I figured I might get lucky and be able to hitch a ride with somebody I knew.

Which I did.

I hadn't more than reached the county road, when here came Larry Lief in his van, and I knew him pretty well because I knew his sister Megan. I stuck out my thumb, and he stopped, and I hopped in. "Give me a ride into town?"

"Certainly," he said. "How's your folks?"

"Okay." I was looking at his profile and trying to decide whether I'd ever seen anybody better looking. It wasn't easy, but it sure was fun.

"I was out at your place just the other day," he told me. "You've got a nice mother."

It was a big lie, but I thought he was just being polite, so I said, "Sure." Maybe my voice wasn't quite what it ought to have been.

We stopped for a light, and he looked around at me. "You deserve one," he said; and then, "We don't always get what we've got coming, Holly. None of us." Then he switched on the radio.

Right here I want to write that I forgot it almost as soon as it happened; but I guess I didn't, really. Larry wasn't just being polite when he said that, and I knew it. Ever since he'd gotten out of the army and come back to Barton to live with his folks, I'd known that Megan and his wife, Molly, thought he had big problems, just from the way they talked about him. But I think that was the first time I'd really realized they weren't just worrying over nothing. It isn't too easy for somebody that good-looking to look down, but I was still thinking about Larry and how down he'd looked while I hiked across the parking lot and up the steps to the CW&N station.

There was only one other person waiting for the ten o'clock train, a guy at least ten years older than I was. I noticed him because he turned for just a second to give me the once-over as I came up, and he had a once-over like I didn't think anybody *could* have. It didn't take long at all, but I felt like I could hear the shutters click. Those eyes had me cold, and he'd know me again if he met me in the New Guinea jungle twenty years from now.

After that, naturally, I looked at *him*. Those two little camera lenses were bright blue and set quite a ways behind the rest of his face, which was bony. There was a high, squarish, almost narrow forehead, and straw-blond hair in a widow's peak. It was getting pretty thin, and the rest of him was thin already—in fact, he was one of the skinniest people I had ever seen. One leg was stiff; he had one of those plain wooden broom-handle canes that they sell in drugstores, and it looked old. He was wearing khaki work pants and a white office shirt, open at the throat and rolled up past the elbows. He had a little trouble getting onto the train when it came, and that's when I made my mistake, or anyway what I thought for a while was a mistake.

(Really I don't make many mistakes, because I've found out that if you just yell at a mistake long enough it will usually straighten itself around and turn into some kind of shrewd move—like the time I broke my leg and got out of gym and my father promised to buy me the horse that turned out to be Sidi.)

Anyway there I was, the little Girl Scout, trying to catch hold of the cane so I could help him up. He could have done it okay by himself, but anyway (I guess because he wanted to show he was grateful) he went down to the smoking car with me and sat down next to me. He smells cleaner than anybody else I know—like he's washed himself all over with lye soap. You don't ask where anybody's going on a CW&N commuter, because everybody's going to Chicago, so I said, "Going shopping?"

"No. Just going to try to collect a few bad debts. You?"

I said I was going to see a sick relative, which I thought was very clever of me at the time, and we got to talking. After a while, because it was on my mind, I guess, I asked whether he knew anything about bus service to Dawn.

He laughed, surprised, and said, "Oh, you're going to Dawn? That's quite a coincidence—so am I. How's your uncle?"

And before I could think about what I was saying, I said, "How'd you know about him?"

"Herbert Hollander is your uncle? I thought so."

"We always keep this really quiet," I told him. "Have you been talking to Mrs. Maas?" My mind was going round and round, because it looked like pretty soon this would be worse than if I'd taken her Ford.

He laughed again (he has a good laugh, the kind you'd like in the audience if you were a comedian) and winked and said, "I have spies everywhere!"

"Do you know my father?"

He shook his head. "I wish I did. I've seen him on the street, just as I've seen you, but we've never spoken."

"You know my mother, then."

"I have several friends who know your mother. One is the shampoo boy at Felice's."

"He told you?"

He shook his head. "I doubt that your mother's small talk under the drier contains many references to Herbert Hollander."

"Then how did you know?"

He smiled and turned away like he didn't want me to see it. We were already past the golf course, and the trees and fields of the greenbelt were giving up the ghost (an Indian ghost, I suppose) to suburban houses. When he looked back at me he said, "You seem an intelligent young woman. Surely you can guess by now?"

"How could I possibly? I don't have the facts."

"You mean you lack an exhaustive list of my acquaintances. If you had one it would do you no good, only confuse you. If you can't guess without that sort of information, you couldn't possibly guess if you were burdened with it."

I'm good at a lot of things, but there's one I'm not worth a damn at, and that's turning on the feminine charm to get what I want out of a man. I tried it then, leaning over and catching hold of his arm and making my eyes go all misty while I said, "Please? Because I helped you?"

He just about laughed in my face. "Believe me, that's not the way. You should have said, 'Because I need your help.' Or at least you should have if you really required the information. You've been watching television. It turns people into idiots about human relations."

"I don't watch *that* kind of TV. Listen, I really do need your help."

"Much better. Why?"

"Because Elaine—because my mother and father feel very, very strongly about this Uncle Bert thing, and if it gets out they'll think I was the one who told. I have to know who did tell, so I can point the finger."

"Me."

"You've already told other people?"

He was smiling again. "Not really. But I might. I doubt, though, that your parents will think of you. They probably don't even know you know."

"Yes, they do. My father told me. Now please tell me who told you."

"You really do feel you have to find out, don't you? All right, I'll answer your question. But a professional man has to turn a profit. So in exchange for my information, I want you to give me frank and honest answers to two questions of my own, and grant me a favor."

"What's the favor? Who are you, anyway?"

"That's two more questions, which makes it three to three. The favor is that you let me go to the bus with you, and ride out to Dawn and up to Garden Meadow with you. Until you helped me into this train, I hadn't realized how much I've missed the company of pretty women. As to who I am, here's my card."

He took it from his shirt pocket, but it still looked new—not a fancy engraved one like my father's but not a cheapie either. It read:

ALADDIN BLUE
Criminologist

with a Barton post-office box and a South Barton (I could tell by the exchange) phone number. I stuck it in my shirt pocket. "Is that your real name?"

"No more questions from you. I've answered two of yours already, including telling you what the favor I want is. Is it a deal?"

I nodded.

"Then answer one of mine. What do you know about your Uncle Herbert?"

"Everything?"

"Yes. Everything."

"All right. Uncle Bert—he's really Herbert Hollander the Third—is Father's big brother. He's about six or seven years older, I think. He's crazy. You know that, too; if he wasn't he wouldn't be in Garden Meadow, which is a sort of hospital for crazy people."

"Rich crazy people," Aladdin Blue put in.

"Right. It costs a couple of thousand a month just to keep him there. One time I heard my father say it was like sending a kid to college, only worse; and it never stops. He doesn't talk much about things that happened when he was a kid, and I think the reason is that Uncle Bert would be in all the stories. They must've been pretty close, and maybe he joined the army when he was young because Uncle Bert was in it already. Uncle Bert was a captain."

17

"But now your father is rich, and your uncle is poor."

It wasn't a question, just a statement thrown out for me to let pass if I wanted to, but I could tell from the way he said it that he knew something already—maybe more than I did. "Not exactly," I said. "My grandfather—he was Herbert Hollander, Junior—was kind of a nut, in one way anyhow."

"He founded the Hollander Safe and Lock Company and made a fortune."

"Right, but he was kind of a nut just the same. He had a partner when he started, and there was a lot of trouble between them."

"I didn't know that," Blue said.

"He bought this partner out pretty early, while the company was still small, but I guess he always remembered those fights and felt that they could have done a lot better if he'd been the only boss."

"And—?"

"And so when he died he left my father some money. But he left all the stock in the company to Uncle Bert, because he was older. My father had been working for the company, too. He was a vice president, and because he'd been doing a good job Uncle Bert kept him on. Then when Uncle Bert had his breakdown, the court made my father his guardian. It seems like when a person goes crazy, they don't take their property away, it's just like the person was a kid."

"But if your uncle recovered, he'd be able to take control of his company again."

"Yeah, only I don't think that's going to happen. Because another thing I know about Uncle Bert—I believe this's the last one—is that he's still in Garden Meadow and he's pretty sick. That's why I'm going to see him now. Are you going to tell me why you want to know all this?"

"Because I knew some of it already. It's an odd situation, and I'm insatiably curious by nature. You wanted to know how I knew as much as I did, but as I said, it should've been obvious from what you already knew. I didn't learn it from you, or from your father or mother—who have, I'd say, excellent reasons for keeping it quiet. By the way, you were supposed to give me all the information you had about your uncle. You referred to him as 'crazy' but never told me what his insanity consisted of. Do you know?"

I shook my head. "I've never heard—or even thought about it."

"Then we'll let that pass for now. As I said, the source of my information should have been clear to you almost from the beginning. I'm going to Garden Meadow, too, to visit a friend. My friend—he's Judge Bain, of whom you may have heard—"

"I thought he was in jail."

Blue nodded. "The judge was sent up in connection with a racing scandal, but when his grasp of reality failed, and he was transferred to a state hospital for the criminally insane, the governor commuted his sentence. His family sent him to Garden Meadow, where he's become quite a crony of your Uncle Herbert's. He's a charming man, the old judge, and they must be nearly the same age. Understandably, your uncle doesn't feel obligated to conceal his ownership of Hollander Safe and Lock."

"You're right," I said. "I should've guessed."

"Now for my last question. Answer this, and we're even. What's in Pandora's Box?"

3

How I Lost Every Cent
and Had to Hitch

IT was like a spa, if you can imagine what a spa would be
like if every guest stayed a long, long time—a big old three-
story house, part limestone and part wood, with pillars in
front and a lobby with chairs and books and a big TV. The
main difference between the staff and the patients seemed
to me to be that the patients had better clothes but looked—
most of them—a little sloppy.

A nurse took Blue right up to see his friend the judge like
they'd been expecting him; but he'd made a phone call from
the station in Chicago, and I've always figured that was why
and he hadn't been going there until I'd said I was. I had
to go in to talk to Uncle Bert's doctor, which I had expected,
and he tried to phone our house, which I hadn't. But when
Mrs. Maas told him my mother and father were both gone,
he decided to let me go up. I was cussing myself for not
having worn a nice dress and more lipstick; if I had I could
have passed for twenty-one and there wouldn't have been
any trouble. But everything worked out okay. Be yourself,

as TV guys who spent two hours in makeup are always telling us.

Uncle Bert had a big room with three windows on the second floor, but as soon as I saw him he stopped being Uncle Bert for me and turned into Herbert Hollander III to stay, or at least no chummier than Uncle Herbert. He looked a little like my father, but not much. My father's what people call a tall man, around six foot one or two, I guess. Uncle Herbert was six five or six easy, but stooped. He was quite a bit thinner, too. His hair was starting to go, and what was left was white; but he moved around almost like the guys on the hardball team, and if I'd had to pick the winner in a fistfight between him and my father, I'm not so sure I wouldn't have picked him. He was wearing one of those really wild black-and-red sportcoats you see now and then, with a bright blue knit shirt and white slacks. There was wire over the windows, but for all you could tell it might have been there to keep the pigeons out.

"So you're Harry's little girl," he said, and took hold of my hands. The doctor had phoned a male nurse on this floor and told him I was coming up.

I said, "Call me Holly," wondering whether he was going to let go of me or try something.

He let go. "That's fine, Holly. Fine. Sit down, won't you?" There were a couple of armchairs besides the bed and a dresser, both with tapestry seats and back, and ball-and-claw legs.

I sat. "How're you feeling, Uncle Herbert?"

"So they've told you about me, and that's why you've come. Certainly, certainly. I feel perfectly fit, Holly. Would you believe I played a round of golf this morning? We've a nine-hole course, and I think that I might win the National Open, if only it were played here. I know every bush and hummock."

I said that was good, and we made quite a bit of small

21

talk, me telling him all about Sidi and school and so forth, and him asking me about my father and Elaine. He'd never ridden a jet, he said, and he was surprised when I said I'd gone to Chicago on the train, because TV and magazines had given him the impression that there were only freight trains left.

Then he got off onto prices, and he asked so many questions that I thought, uh-oh, here it comes, pretty soon he'll get mad or start singing or something.

Except he never did. He was amazed at how much everything cost, and talked a lot about how the government was selling out the country, but everybody does that, and I've heard people in our living room get a lot madder than he was. He wanted to know how much his sportcoat had cost at Marshall Field's, but I could only guess at it because I don't know much about men's clothes. Then he wanted to know how much it cost to ride the train (a dollar eighty-five back then, if you're curious) and how much a cheap meal might be. So I told him how much at McDonald's for a shake and a Big Mac with fries, and then I had to tell him all about McDonald's, the golden arches and all that.

When I was about to go he kissed my hand, bowing from the hips the way he had, I guess, been taught to in dancing school about 1929. It made me feel funny. Then he took both my hands like he had when I'd first come and asked me if I could give him some money. I started to say that my father had just been there—which he had, because Uncle Herbert had told me—and he could have given him whatever he needed. Then I thought, well, if he were really on the ball about all this he wouldn't be in Garden Meadow, now would he? And probably by asking me for money he's testing me, and the money represents love to him. I've got my return train ticket, and even if that Aladdin Blue guy doesn't have a whole lot of cash, he'd probably help me out and I could pay him back.

but the ones who are sincere in trying to understand themselves, and have something real to understand."

"Like you," I said, but I don't think he heard me.

"Most people outside, particularly most successful people outside, don't really have problems in any serious sense. I myself was a successful person, Holly dear, on the outside. I inherited the company, but I quadrupled our volume during the five—or five and a half, or whatever it was—years that I ran things. I met a great many of the men at the top during those years, and I can testify that the men at the top are rather dull."

I said I'd always suspected that.

"You're a very perceptive girl. They are all of one piece. A few are brilliant, but even the brilliant ones are hardly more than thinking machines. They have their lives in order, and no errant impulse ever disturbs their days, which may be frantic in many instances, yet are tranquil nonetheless. They have reached their positions because they have been able to keep a single end in view for well over half their lives, that end being authority within a very narrowly defined structure."

"I don't think I could do that," I told him.

"In all probability you won't have to, my dear," he said. "And so you will be spared a great many dull meetings. . . . I was talking toward something, I'm certain, but I've forgotten what it was. Perhaps I intended to say that we failures—and we are all failures here, of one sort or another—are the fascinating ones, each of us more people than you will find in many plays, all done up in a single skin. No, that wasn't it."

"You were saying this was a real Paradise, Uncle Herbert. Only I've got to get going."

He took my hand. His own hand was bigger and harder than my father's, I suppose from all the golf. "I feel the same way myself, Holly. They have it all wrong, you know, the ones who think that they're divine. They're always saying that sinners shall be cast into hell when they die, and the just lifted up to heaven. I did a terrible thing, and I was dropped into Paradise while I lived. Nobody should live in Paradise, Holly. It is for the dead." He put both big hands on my shoulders and kissed my cheek. "I'm pissing blood—did they tell you? You will come back, won't you?"

Lying through my teeth I said, "I sure will, Uncle Herbert."

He nodded, and I got the feeling that I hadn't fooled him for a second; but all he said was, "Until I see you again."

I had to sign out and everything, and when I did I saw that Blue had left about half an hour ahead of me, taking the little jitney bus that stopped at Garden Meadow on its way to Dawn. I had my train ticket all right, and forty-two cents change, but no way to pay for the jitney, and even if they had trusted me, no way to pay for the Greyhound from Dawn to Chicago. The year before I'd always carried a five in my bra, and that was my mad money. Then everybody at school quit wearing them, so I spent the five on a movie with Les. Now thanks to Gloria You-know-who and Kate You-know-who and so forth, there I was outside Garden Meadow sticking my thumb out and wishing I had a hat to push my bonny brown locks up into. Well, it always works like a charm for those faire maids of Shakespeare's.

In a way it was kind of interesting and taught me a lot about myself, the sort of stuff Uncle Herbert had been talking about. Because when I first got out on the shoulder with my thumb, I wasn't going to take a ride with anybody who didn't look a whole lot like me, and by the time I had been hitching a while I would have climbed into an old pickup with Igor and Dr. Frankenstein. Only what I really got was a salesman, a woman gym teacher, and then another salesman. The first two worked me so hard about how dangerous it was to hitchhike that I turned it around and worked the second salesman, telling him how he could get his throat cut picking up wild kids like me. By the time we got past the Oldsmobile place in Barton I could see him thinking about pulling right up to the police station. But in the end he won it fair and square, letting me out at the corner of Main and Half Street, where the stoplight is. By that time I was trying so hard not to laugh that I had practically forgotten about my crazy uncle and losing all my bread.

4
How I Saw the Black Sedan
But Not Larry

WHILE I was hiking up our private road I caught sight of a green van parked in front of our house. Yes, the exact same van (what an astounding coincidence!) with *Magic Key of Barton* on the side that I'd hitched a ride to town in. So naturally, genius that I am, I figured Megan had come over and wanted to Do Something; so I hollered and ran into the house.

Nobody was there. Nobody at all.

I checked the family room, which would have been where Mrs. Maas or Elaine would have dumped Megan, then my room, thinking she might have gone up there to play some tapes and wait for me. Zilch.

Finally I went through the whole damn house looking for anybody—all the bedrooms and the kitchen and the dumb little storeroom Elaine always called the butler's pantry. Nothing.

I stuck my nose into the study, too, because I figured that was the one room where nobody, not even Bill, would take her, so naturally she'd be there. Naturally she wasn't.

So then I thought, well, I'll just take a look at the box, because that guy Blue was so anxious to find out what's in it, and I felt like a dummy telling him I didn't know. Maybe I can even figure out how to get the damned thing open.

I poked around for a minute before I remembered that Elaine had said somebody from the bank was coming out today to pick it up and put it in their window as part of the hype for the Fair. My father locked the study door a lot, so sometimes the cleaning lady and Mrs. Maas didn't get in to vacuum and wipe off all the furniture and stuff like they should have, and I could still see exactly where Pandora's Box had been sitting on the big library table, a ghost of its shape in the dust.

But the whole room felt funny somehow, like something else was missing. At first I thought it was just the box, but really I'd only been in there twice when it was there, as nearly as I could remember—when Bill lugged it in and that morning when I'd gone in to sneak a peek at the letter. Finally I decided it was just because the house was so quiet.

So you can bet it was just then that I heard a door close someplace, and if you come around asking about a certain teenage hellcat who practically jumped right out of her harness boots, I'll be able to show her to you straight off.

I suppose you've got it all figured out that this being the kind of story it is, why naturally that door was being closed by a syndicate hit man at the very least. Wrong. It was only Mrs. Maas, and when I asked her what the heck was going on, she said "Mrs. Hollander" (my mother Elaine to you and me) had asked her to pick up a few things at the drugstore, and she had taken the opportunity to do a little grocery shopping. I looked through the "things" and told her Elaine practically never went in the water. It sailed right over Mrs. Maas's head, but it started me thinking about Garden Meadow again. I wished I could have asked her about Uncle Herbert, who I was nearly ready to start calling Uncle Bert again. Only Barton isn't exactly Pippington-on-the-Squeak, where all those nice English ladies drop arsenic in the tea and stab dubious women with Florentine daggers. . . .

(Hey, I don't mean to change the subject all of a sudden, but hasn't it ever struck you that if the Secretary of Defense was really smart he'd issue those Florentine daggers to all the combat marines? I think I've read a dozen books where somebody gets it with a Florentine dagger, and none of them even twitched afterward. Today I read in the *News* where a sixty-nine-year-old retired machinist got beat over the head with a beer bottle and slashed and stabbed with a big hunting knife, and after the guys had taken his wallet and split, he made it to the emergency ward on foot.)

Anyway as I was saying, in Barton we haven't got those old family retainers who remember when Sir Rollo was but a wee tyke. Mrs. Maas had only been with us about four years and Bill less than two, so if I wanted to hear old family stories I'd have to make them up or ask the folks.

So I said, "Where's Dad?" and Mrs. Maas told me she didn't know, he'd gone out in the morning and hadn't come back. (That would be to Garden Meadow, but he must have stopped somewhere on the way home.) So then I asked, "Where's Elaine?" and Mrs. Maas said, "She was here when I left."

No matter what my old math teacher may have told you, I'm a gritty brat who hangs right in there. I said, "What was Larry Lief doing here?" and she said, "Who's Larry Lief?"

Strikeout.

Then she said, "Oh, is he that good-looking blond man who wears coveralls? About twenty-five?"

"He's Megan's brother," I told Mrs. Maas, "and I'm pretty sure he's quite a bit older than that."

"Well, Mr. Lief's been here several times to talk with Mrs. Hollander about Pandora's Box. He's the one who's going to open it, you know, at the Fair, when they have the drawing."

HOW I SAW THE BLACK SEDAN BUT NOT LARRY

I hadn't. But it made sense, because Larry was a locksmith and ran the only lock shop in Barton, the only one I knew about anyway, and since his shop hadn't been open that long, he could probably use the publicity. I figured my father could have done it about as well, but that would have made it look like too much of a Hollander Family deal maybe, and besides you couldn't ever count on him to be around; if there was trouble at some company and he was on the board he might have to fly to Algiers on about an hour's notice. He could have loaned the Fair an expert from his plant, sure, but the plant's way to hell and gone down below Gary.

Anyway I wandered out to the garage, just hanging around, thinking that the Caddy would be gone. But the Caddy was right there shined up like a wet seal, and Bill was in his room above the garage reading a comic. And Larry's van *was* gone, having started up without my hearing it while I was looking around the house, probably before Mrs. Maas came back, because she hadn't said anything about it. Okay, I'm hip.

So I went over to our little pasture, caught Sidi (not very hard because by that time I had a couple of lumps of sugar in my pocket), saddled up, and *Hi-Yo!*

Since I wasn't going to catch a train or anything, I rode him right into town. There are two liquor stores in Barton, a big one and a little one; the big one's My Case, at the corner of Main and Woly. Woly's just a grotty little dead-end street that folds when it bumps into the CW&N right-of-way, but there's a string of shops down one side of it behind the liquor store: the Redman Lounge, one of the very few spots in Barton where you (you, not me) can buy a drink, the Whileaway Travel Agency, the Magic Key, and so on. I tied Sidi to a parking meter (no ticket for me, because where would the meter maid put it, right?) and went in.

I guess locks run in the Hollander blood; one of these days I'll get in the business if I have to open a deli. That was a joke, but it's really the truth about locks. They're nice and solid, and they've got this shine to them and snap with a good, solid *chink*. There's not much plastic even about the cheap ones you have to buy for your locker at school, and the classy ones have more class than any car I've ever seen. What I'm trying to say, I guess, is that I always liked the Magic Key. It wasn't one of those bright places like a chain drugstore, and it wasn't dim like the Wicker Works. It was dim in places and bright in others, which I think is how a store should be, and it smelled a little bit of sewing-machine oil, which is okay with me. A lot of my friends go for incense, and it's a great cover-up for pot; but I think incense belongs in church.

"*You!*" somebody yelled. "Put that down unless you're going to buy it."

I turned around—I'd picked up one of those fancy gadgets you snap on to keep your sister-in-law from calling Nome on your touch-tone phone—and naturally it was Megan, sticking out her lip trying to look tough. Molly was there, too, working on the books or something behind the counter.

Molly was Larry's wife. She was from some little place the other side of Nashville, and it was my opinion that if somebody thought she was pretty that somebody'd make a pretty good truck driver. Basically what she had was one of those thin poor-li'l-me hillbilly faces, with lots of yellow hair as puffy as cotton candy (and as sticky, too, I'd bet) piled up on top, and a shape like a sack of grapefruit.

Now that I've got that out of my system, I ought to be fair and tell some good stuff about her. Even though she could stop the average heavy construction job dead in its tracks, she knew she wasn't pretty. You could see it in her eyes and the way she held herself when she thought nobody was looking, and as far as I was concerned that was ten points in her favor. The teasing and all that hair spray were just her dim-bulb way of trying to *get* pretty, so you had to feel sorry for her. And she tried to be nice to Megan and me, so who cared if she was really too old to be buddy-buddy? Also, she did her best to sit on her accent. She didn't succeed very well, but you could tell she was trying, and I've got to give her more points for that; I'm not going to spell out the way she really talked, or at least not very often. Megan said that Larry had met Molly while he was stationed down south after his second tour. It was getting married, she said, that made him decide to chuck the army.

"Well," ("Wa-al") "hello, Holly. Haven't seen your smilin' face 'round here for many a day."

"Gosh," I said, "I can't make everybody happy all at once."

Molly and Megan both laughed.

Back then Megan was about my best friend—if not really the best, awfully close to it. Her father owned the Corner Cobbler, which wasn't a shoe-repair shop like it sounds but a shoe store; but the Liefs weren't rich, and when you are (or think that you are) it's hard to get to be best friends with anybody who isn't. I've already described Molly, so I might as well describe Megan, too. She's really pretty, with page-boy blond hair and a perky baby-face that goes just fine with it. I'd have paid a yard at least for those big, bright-blue, dirty-flirty eyes of hers, and nobody's ever called me stone ugly. Her worst feature was her hips, I'd say; Megan's a little wide across the pockets.

"Holly, can't you tell us—just us, we won't tell anybody—what's in that box? *Is it gold?*"

"Stop hissing," I told Megan. "You sound like the radiator on Kris's Mustang."

"I'm playing pirate." Her voice went into a parrot squawk. *"Pieces o' eight! Pieces o' eight!"*

"Well," ("Wa-al") "it could be gold, couldn't it, Holly? I believe I'm goin' to go. Maybe they'll pick my name."

"They're going to draw by number," I told Molly. "And for all I know it could be chock-full of diamonds—it's plenty heavy enough. It could also be full of rocks. Elaine got it at some junk shop. She says they didn't have a key and didn't want to bust it open."

"Whatever 'tis, it's mine. That sign in the bank's got me purely fascinated."

"You birds busy now?"

"I am. I got to watch out for things here. But you and Megan can go traipsin' off if you want to."

"I'm learning the business," Megan explained. "Larry says if I do he might put me on the payroll."

So Larry had come up without me even having to do it. When you're hot, you're hot. Naturally I asked, "Where's Larry now, anyhow?"

Did you ever make some innocent little remark that laid the festivities stone cold? You know, "My, my, what's *that* doing in the punch bowl?" And nobody says, "Looks like the backstroke," because there really *is* something in the punch that ought to be in the zoo. Sure you have, so you know just how I felt. Megan quit smiling, and for a second there I thought Molly was going to cry. Her face had a sort of spasm.

Megan said, "He's in South Barton someplace. Changing the locks to keep sombody's ex-wife out."

"Something's the matter, huh?" (Subtle's my middle name.)

"Oh, someone's been phoning for him, and Molly's a little scared about it."

"I don't believe it amounts to cow flop," Molly said, and the way she said it you could tell she was worried stiff.

"Who is this someone?"

"They won't give no name."

Megan said, "He only calls when Larry's gone. Or if he calls when Larry's here Larry won't admit he talked to him."

"What's he say?"

"Nothin'." That was Molly.

"He just says, 'Let me speak to Sergeant Lief.' When we say Larry's not here, he hangs up."

"Sergeant Lief? I thought Larry was a lieutenant."

Molly stood up and smoothed her dress, looking proud for a minute. "He was a sergeant first, Holly. It was what they call a battlefield commission."

"It's not what this guy says," Megan put in. "It's the way he sounds. Sometimes when I hear him, I wonder whether Larry's coming back at all." She looked at Molly. "I guess I shouldn't have said that."

I didn't think she should have either. Molly wasn't strong on lips at the best of times, and when Megan came out with that beauty her mouth looked like the cut a can opener makes. She reached down under the counter by the cash register and came up with a .38 snub-nose, not pointing it at us but just laying it there on the glass and turning it around and around with one long bright-red fingernail. "Maybe I never went to no college, but I witness that I learned to shoot from my brothers, and it was a hard school. You might want to pass it around town that the day Larry don't come home somebody else won't eat no supper either."

"You put that away before you get us all busted," I said. The Barton cops are damn near afraid to touch their own guns.

Molly picked up the revolver again and held it, weighing it in her hand. "You tell them what will happen if sometime Larry don't come home," she said; but after a second or two she stuck it back under the register.

"How long have you been learning the business?" I asked Megan, trying to pretend that nothing had happened.

"Two hours, maybe."

"Then come on before you suffer terminal brain-strain. I need you to help me pass judgment on a new blow-drier."

It must have sounded retarded as hell, but Molly wasn't the type to notice; hair was serious business for her, and it let me pull Megan out of the shop.

When she was up behind me on Sidi she whispered, "He names guys sometimes, and then he gives a year. Corporal

35

Raglan, nineteen seventy-two. Like that. It isn't just that, either. I think he's told Molly that Larry's got another girl someplace."

I guess my face must have looked about like Molly's had in the shop; it's a damned good thing Megan couldn't see it. "She know who it is?"

Megan said no, and reeled off a list of suspects, none of them Elaine. By the time she got to the end I wasn't paying a whole lot of attention. Across from the Redman Lounge a black sedan was pulling away from the curb, and I hadn't seen anybody get into it.

5

How Uncle De Witte Sinclair
Played Postman

MAYBE this is where I should write a transition. You
know, "The big yellow summer sun grew brighter each new
day. Me and Leslie and Megan, and Kris and Adam and
John lolled around our pool and Les's pool and the pool in
the park. Locusts buzzed in the elms like spaced-out door-
bells, and the hamburger smell from the fast-food joints up
on the highway came drifting through the shadows like
smoke."

There—I knew I could do it. What I'm really trying to
say is that summer dragged along about like it usually does.
On TV, reruns of utterly ghastly shows got pushed aside by
first runs of the most utterly god-awful summer tryouts the
world has ever seen. I went on strike about Elaine wanting
me to drop karate. Everybody was sick to death of movies,
but it wasn't nearly time to think about the homecoming
dance yet.

What it *was* time to think of, naturally, was the Fair. And
all of us got mixed up in it one way or another. We were
all so bored we would have mixed into a sparrow fight.

I guess it was a good thing; Lord knows there was plenty of donkey work to do. There were cards you had to talk the stores and eateries into sticking up in their windows, envelopes by the thousand to address and stuff, and the whole damned high school to get ready. I think I already mentioned that there was always a book sale. It was put on by the Friends of the Barton Public Library, which is not the same as the Women's Club, though a lot of people belong to both of them. The Friends is supposed to be for men as well as women, and there are actually some men in it—seven or eight the last time I looked. Also there are kids in it, because all the librarians belong and if you hang around the library very much they bring you coffee and cookies from their Common Room and talk a little about the Greatest Writer in the World (meaning whoever you just discovered that you didn't think anybody else knew about; for me then it was Baroness Blixen, or maybe the Englishman who wrote the Father Brown mysteries) and first thing you know they're shoving a piece of paper in front of your nose.

Then you say, "Oh, gee. Well, gosh, it's fifteen bucks a year. Honest, Ms. Sudden, I *don't have* fifteen bucks."

Then Ms. Sudden, who's gone through this maybe fifty times and probably gets a new chain for her glasses whenever she signs up another kid, says, "Darling, don't worry about a thing. The Friends will just send a bill to your home, and I'm certain your parents will be delighted that you want to become involved."

Now right there was where she slipped it past you. *Become involved.* That means that when the book sale looms over the old horizon the Friends are going to call you up, and next thing you know you're bouncing along in the back of a truck with four or five other slave-labor kids, heading for a house you never knew existed down at the end of a dirt road to load up a hundred tons of books some lady's father left behind when he passed on during the Coolidge inauguration.

"Oh, dear," says the old lady. "I didn't know you'd bring so many children with you."

Tom Coffey, who's doing this because his wife Willa's big in the Friends and he owns the truck, says, "Ma'am, you said you had several sizable boxes, and we didn't want to keep you long."

"Well," says the old lady, "it's terribly hot, and I don't suppose your truck is air conditioned," (it doesn't even have a top over the back) "so why don't you and the children come in and have some ice tea first?"

And that's the way it goes. At this particular place I'm thinking of, we all trooped in—me feeling the wall to make sure it wasn't gingerbread, I know my way around—and sweated all over her furniture, and laughed, and got to see a real tea ball made out of copper, which was something I'd read about but never seen before. (Mrs. Maas used Nestle's Instant mix.) I told the old lady she ought to exhibit it at the Fair, and she said, "Do you really think so? Maybe I'll come down this year and have a look." So I'd gotten Elaine's Fair another customer.

Then we toted the boxes out—fourteen, and some so heavy it took two to lift them. Right on top I saw Dreiser and Hemingway and *Java Head,* by Joseph Hergesheimer, and a bound volume of *The Smart Set.* The old lady's daddy must have been some dude.

But the part I really wanted to tell about came when we got back up on the truck. We stacked her books on top of the stuff we had already picked up at some other places and sat on top of that, which put us up pretty high. From there I could see over the bushes and stuff; the house was on a hill and when I looked down between the nearest trees, the rest sort of fell away in a long wave, like the surf the time we went to Great Abaco Island. It was really beautiful. Away far away I could see this little white dot of building, almost like I was looking out the window of a plane, with this neat little black road running in front of it and bright green lawns all around it. And I thought: that's the place! That's where I want to be!

So I stuck my elbow in Les and said, "Lookit that! What do you suppose it is?"

And Les said, "That's Barton High, you dummy."

Ah, romance! That was exactly where we were going with our load of books, because they were setting up the Friends' Book Sale in the chem lab, and Uncle De Witte Sinclair would be there to price them.

Uncle Dee wasn't really my uncle, like Uncle Bert—that's just what I called him because my father told me to when I was an itty brat. I ought to tell you about him because he's sort of important to this story. But it's going to be hard because about anything you could say about Uncle Dee that was true made him sound like an awful bastard. Except when you actually knew him, you didn't think he was a bastard, you liked him a lot. At least I did, and I think quite a few people did; if they hadn't, he'd have been flat broke.

Uncle Dee must have been at least sixty and maybe more, but his face was so smooth he looked, sometimes, like a much younger guy in makeup. He had bright blue eyes and bushy white eyebrows, and white hair so long and thick they'd put him in the Senate if he just walked through the door. His business was rare books, and I honestly didn't know if he was rich or poor. He had a big house in Barton Hills, with rooms where his customers could look at his stock. Still, you never could tell—some people with big houses in Barton Hills were in bankruptcy court. And I ask you, rare books? Anyhow, I think Uncle Dee had been driving the same rusty Chevy and wearing the same old tweed suit with the leather elbow patches ever since I'd known him, which was around twelve years plus.

My father collected books about—you guessed it—safes and locks, and he used to say he could tell when Uncle Dee had found something really good, because then Uncle Dee would call him up and invite him out to his house.

When it was only so-so, he'd come over to ours, usually with two or three things, and he and my father would talk about books and locks and The Great Houdini and so on for a couple of hours and have a couple of drinks, and then Uncle Dee would pull out an old magazine with a story that Houdini was supposed to have written, although both of them knew (but I bet you didn't) that Houdini's stories were ghosted by a man in Rhode Island.

Naturally they would yak about that for an hour or so, and maybe my father would pay twenty or thirty for it and maybe he wouldn't. Then Uncle Dee would come up with something else and ask a hundred and maybe take forty or fifty. So, you say, who needs a friend like that? The fact is that my father did. He was never so relaxed or in such a good mood as when Uncle Dee finally started up his old car, unless maybe it was when he got back from spending an evening at Uncle Dee's. All right, it cost him a couple of hundred bucks, but I've seen people spend a lot more and get a lot less. Sure he loved Elaine—in fact, he was so absolutely silly about her that sometimes I kind of thought he'd have burned the house down with me inside just to see her smile. But that was only because she was so damn beautiful and so much younger than he was; in person, if you know what I mean, she drove him bananas. His collection in the study and his shop in the basement, and Uncle Dee, were what kept him from turning on the gas.

Anyway what Uncle did was go to garage sales and grungy old secondhand shops around Chicago and everywhere else where there might be old books. He'd look through a thousand tons of junk hoping to find a first edition of *Tamerlane,* which is by Edgar Allan Poe but doesn't say so. Only what he'd really find would be a certain book written in 1890 by a particular lady who came to Chicago for the summer, and he'd buy it and sooner or later sell it to a customer who collected books about Chicago. That old magazine he sold my father for thirty bucks probably cost him fifty cents, and one way to look at that is that it's an awfully skuggy way to make a living.

Just the same, there are a couple of other ways to look at it, too.

Like I said, Uncle Dee went through a mountain of garbage to find that magazine for my father, and these days even garbage men pull down ten bucks an hour. What's more, Uncle Dee was one of the few people I've ever met who never tried to get paid when he hadn't done the job. He never came to our house and said, "I looked all day for something for you, Harry, but there wasn't a damn thing, so how about fifty bucks for my trouble?" Uncle Dee told everybody he was from Richmond, Virginia, but sometimes I wondered if he was really American at all, because I've noticed that most of the other guys who never try to chisel you are wetback Mexican busboys.

Besides, Uncle Dee loved his books, and I think that when he bought one for two bucks and sold it for two hundred he felt like the hero who finds The Lost Prince of Graustark slopping hogs and puts him on the throne. He felt that book was *worth* a couple of hundred, or maybe more, and he, crafty old Uncle De Witte Sinclair, was restoring it to its God-given position in society. Part of the time he must have been right; and when he priced old books for the Friends, I don't think he ever marked anything too low so he could buy it cheap, even though maybe sometimes he was tempted.

So when I came in lugging my box and saw him there in the dusty smell of all those books with his wide smile and his soft lead pencil, I put down the box and put my arms around him and gave him a good smooch. Because that was another thing about Uncle Dee—white hair or not, he still liked girls. He wasn't a pincher or a pawer (if he had been I would have kept a mile out of his reach) but when he turned on that southern-fried charm he was doing it for the same reason he had when he was seventeen, and wasn't just going though the motions. I've seen him look at Elaine like a stray dog at a ham bone plenty of times, and you can bet she never gave him a big kiss and little squeeze to show him life was still worth living.

"Holly, my fairest flower," he said, "how very good to see you! What a coincidence, and what a lovely surprise. So you've enlisted in our little project. You all are doing a wonderful job."

"I'm a member now and everything, Uncle Dee," I told him. "Gonna run for president next year. Vote the straight Hollander ticket."

He shook his finger at me. "You'd better mind your P's and Q's, young lady, or we'll elect you. Think of the pickle you'd be in then." Uncle Dee had been president of the Friends two or three times already, and always said he wouldn't do it anymore.

"So how are they going, and how come it's a coincidence to see me?"

"Quite nicely. One would think that holding this little affair each year as we do the springs would eventually run dry, but someone must be printing old books." It was a regular joke of his, and he was the only one I ever heard laugh at it. "Look here: A.W. Sprague's *Log of the Cruise of the Schooner Julius Webb*. Fifty dollars, and cheap at the price. And here's one I found hardly a minute before you came in: Jim Gillet's *Six Years with the Texas Rangers*. I've put it at sixteen fifty, and I'm going to buy it myself the moment the doors open."

"I might beat you to it—I think I can run faster than you."

His smile would have defrosted a freezer. "That's right, you're getting interested in police and crime books, aren't you? Now here's something you might enjoy that I know you can afford: Franke's *The Torture Doctor*. It's the history of the infamous Chicago murderer H.H. Holmes. No dust jacket, so I've marked it a dollar and a quarter; but you might look for a long time to find a copy, and in a year or two it should be worth ten dollars at least."

He leaned across the table to pick up the book for me, and a piece of loose-leaf paper that had been dangling from his shirt pocket fell out.

"Oh, yes," he said when he got it again, "this is for you, too. A very charming gentleman who said that he was a relation of yours was inquiring after you, not an hour ago. I honestly don't think he realized at first that the school was closed for the summer—no doubt he saw the cars out front and thought a summer semester was in session. I overheard your name and had a little chat with him."

I unfolded the note.

Dear Little Niece,
  Remember what was said under the roses?
  Wear one when you are free to see me.
                    Herbert Hollander III

6

How I Played Carmen to
an Empty House

WELL, what would you have done? Uncle Herbert was crazy, and I had this notion they wouldn't keep somebody locked up so long when he acted as sane as Uncle Herbert did, unless they thought it might be an awfully bad idea to turn him loose. I didn't want to be alone with him, but I didn't want him mad at me either.

And anyhow, where was I supposed to get a rose? Out of the garden, right? Sure. Only there weren't any rose bushes in our garden because it was practically all grass and evergreens, with some redbud trees and ornamental cherries. Besides if I did get a rose, when would I wear it? "Under the roses" meant *sub rosa*—Latin for "on the quiet"—unless I was even dumber than my teachers thought. Naturally Uncle Herbert wanted to keep things as quiet as he could, and that was as open as he'd dared to be about it in a note that a stranger might have read as soon as he was gone. If I wore a rose when there were people around, he might not like it, but if I wore it when I was alone, how could he see it?

In the end, I did two things—maybe smart and maybe not—as soon as we got the rest of the books unloaded and I could sneak away. Boutiques are the curse of Barton, but I found one, the Pink Pelican, that carried paper flowers. I bought a nice red rose, had them put it in a bag, and took it to a phone booth. Then I pulled Aladdin Blue's card out of my wallet and called him up.

After we'd said hello and I'd explained who I was, I said, "That day we went out to Garden Meadow—you knew that my Uncle Herbert was going to bust out, right? That was why you were so interested in him." ·

"I didn't actually know it, Holly." Blue has one of those voices that sound the same over a phone as they do face-to-face. "I'd been told it was probable, yes."

"By your friend the judge?"

"Yes."

"Why didn't you tell me?"

"In the first place, because I had been told in confidence. And in the second, because it would only have worried you to no purpose. What could you have done, if I had? Told the director that your uncle should be watched more carefully? He would have asked you how you knew, and you would have been forced to tell him that you had been warned by a man you met on the train. How much weight would that have carried? He would have assured you that Garden Meadow was extremely secure, and that your uncle was watched quite carefully already."

"I guess you're right," I admitted. "Is it? Secure, I mean?"

"As secure as such places usually are, I imagine, which is slightly less secure than a minimum-security prison. You must understand that out of one hundred psychotics, ninety-nine are dangerous only to themselves. The great risk places like Garden Meadow must guard against is suicide."

"You know he's escaped, too, because when I started talking about it you didn't ask. Can that judge telephone?"

"I suspect he could, if he wanted to badly enough. But

he didn't tell me. I have a police radio, and when I'm working I find it more relaxing than music. The police have a code number to indicate a lost person, and their description fit your uncle quite well."

"I didn't think Garden Meadow would call the police."

"They won't shoot on sight, you understand. Just take him back."

I knew what I wanted to ask next, but I couldn't figure out how to ask it. Finally I said, "When we were on that train, you wanted to know what my uncle had done that got him sent where he was. Or anyhow, you wanted to find out if I knew. Do you know, yourself?"

"He killed his wife," Blue said.

I think I hung up the phone, but I'm not completely sure. The next thing I really remember is walking up the street, about half a block away from the booth. Somebody in my head (I don't know what you call her, except that it isn't Conscience—maybe she's Conscience's sister) was saying, "Okay, Holly, this is it. You know what he looks like, and you know you have to be careful when some other woman wouldn't suspect a thing. Maybe you can con him into going back, and if you can't, you can at least blow the whistle. You've been as cocky as a cat on a cattleboat ever since you were born. Now put up or shut up."

So I stuck the dumb paper rose in my hair—Hey, look at me, I'm Carmen—and went into the Yankeedooodle-Burger joint.

There were lots of people there, but no Uncle Herbert. I was just going to have a Coke and go home, but who did I see in a booth but Megan and Les with Megan's brother Larry, and of course they yelled at me to come over.

"We've got a question," Larry told me. "It's about horses, and you're our horse expert."

Larry was one of the handsomest guys I had ever met; when he looked at me like that I wanted to do whatever he asked me to—even though I knew he was setting me up. So

I said, "Les has two, but I know a lot more than she does."

Les giggled. "He won't take my word on this stuff, Holly. It's up to you to straighten him out."

Megan said, "My smart brother just happened to mention the well-known scientific fact that horses fly south in the winter."

Larry rapped the table. "Let's get this straight. I did not say *fly*. I'm aware that *fly*, when applied to a four-footed animal, is hardly more than a figure of speech. I—"

Naturally they jumped on that. "Bats fly," Les told him. And Megan put in, "What about a hind-footed animal?"

"—merely stated that horses migrate, and I don't intend to be put off by dragged-in references to a dumb animal that spends its time in dugouts."

I figured it was my turn, so I said, "Horses don't migrate, Larry. They gallop, they walk, they trot, they canter, and one or two will even pace—on a good day, with a full moon. But not migrate or swim under water—that's ducks."

"Certainly they do. You, Holly, are shut up in the winter, and so you don't get to observe as I do. But let me tell you a plain, unvarnished fact. I hardly ever see a horse all winter."

"I see one every couple of days," I said, thinking of all the fancy, varnished hours I'd spent mucking out Sidi's stall.

Les added, "And if you'd really looked, right after the big storm in January, you'd have seen the inimitable Hopkins Family Sleigh, drawn by our own dear Big Red."

"Sled horses are scouts," Larry told her, "and it's not at all surprising, Holly, that you saw your horse. He was cooped up, not free to migrate the way Nature intended. Ducks migrate, as you said yourself. When a farmer goes into his poultry house and sees his ducks sitting there, does that prove horses don't migrate?"

Megan corrected him. "You mean ducks, Larry. Ducks don't migrate." That was when I caught onto the fact that Larry was a little high. Okay, I'm slow.

"Certainly they do, sis. Everybody knows that. They can fly, too, some of them."

"Listen," I said, "much as I enjoy all this horsing around, I'd like a Coke and a cheeseburger. 'Scuse me a minute?"

"Me too," Megan said. "But I haven't got any money. How about it, Larry?"

"Okay, but don't let Molly find out I bought three gorgeous women dinner."

What I had really wanted was an excuse that would get me on the other side of the booth, where my back would be to the wall, and for once everything worked out great. We all got up, Larry bought Coke and burgers for Megan and me, a Dr Pepper for Les, and coffee and fries for himself; and when we sat down again, I was in the back corner where I'd be hard to get at, with Larry between me and the table area. I figured that a guy who'd jump out of a helicopter into the jungle with a knife between his teeth should be able to take care of any screwy old uncle, high or not. So that was just fine.

What wasn't fine was that his crack about not letting Molly find out had reminded me of that time I'd come home and seen his truck in front of the house. He and Elaine had split, and where had they split to and how had they done it? I'd looked over the whole house.

Except, come to think of it, I hadn't. I hadn't looked in the shop down in the basement; and besides about a million bucks worth of tools and his lock collection, my father had a nice big couch down there. Sometimes he even slept there—when he didn't want to disturb Elaine, he said, but I think it was really when they'd been fighting and the bedroom was off limits. That day, Elaine might have been afraid Mrs. Maas would come upstairs to make the bed, or she just might not have wanted to take Larry to a messed-up bedroom. The shop would have been perfect, because if they were caught, he could have said he was showing her how he'd open Pandora's Box; and anyway they probably

49

wouldn't have been caught because Mrs. Maas hardly ever went down there, and anybody (such as my father and me) who did go down had to open a door at the top of the steps first, then switch on the little stairway light, and then come down the steps, which were steep and noisy. It would've given them plenty of time to beat it out the door and up the other steps, the concrete ones that went up to the backyard.

So here I was now, sitting close enough to Larry to touch his leg with mine while he kidded away with Megan and Les, and thinking about how he and Elaine must've listened to me walking around upstairs looking for them, and breathed a big sigh when I'd finally gone outside and they could go up the steps and out the front door. Had they gotten back to it, I wondered, parked someplace in Larry's van? But who knows, maybe they were just holding hands. That would've been like Elaine.

"What's the matter?" Megan wanted to know. "Don't you like that cheeseburger?"

"I was thinking," I said. I picked it up and took a bite. It was okay, but I wished I'd remembered to ask them for some of their horseradish sauce. (Do horseradishes migrate?) They keep it for the roast beef, but I like it on burgers. Or at least I did until I realized what it looked like.

And I thought then that if I were just alone with Larry I'd brace him with it. He wasn't exactly a bad guy, and even then I knew enough to know that only one man out of a hundred, married or not, would turn down a woman who looked like Elaine.

"What about?"

"Wondering how the Fair's going to go tomorrow, I guess. Besides, somebody was going to meet me, and I've been looking around for him."

"Kris? Mike?"

I shook my head. "It wasn't definite. I just thought he might show up here." Another bite of burger and a sip of Coke. Thinking, like I said.

And then Megan and Les were saying good-bye, they were going over to Les's, and didn't I want to come?

I said no, I had some things to do in town.

When they had gone, Larry offered me his fries. I don't think he'd touched them, but I shook my head.

"You're pissed off at me, aren't you, Holly? I don't blame you."

That surprised me enough to make me look around at him. "You knew I knew?"

"Elaine said she thought you did."

"I guess I'm not a very good actress. Yeah, I know."

He wouldn't look at me. "So who's hurting, Holly? Maybe I can send a medic."

"I am," I said. "Molly, too, I think."

It took a while, but he finally nodded. "Yeah. Molly. Molly for sure. How do you think Barney feels?"

"I guess I don't know Barney."

"Her first husband. They'd been married eight months when I met her. Let's talk about you. You love your mother, right?"

I shook my head.

"I love her, Holly. Do you believe that? It's true. I've been looking for three or four years now for a woman who wasn't too good for me, that I could love, and I found her. I thought Molly was the one once, but I was wrong. Elaine's as selfish as I am."

"So naturally—" I wanted a sip of Coke but my hand was shaking so bad I had to put it down.

"Yes," Larry said. "*Yes.*"

"Most people don't think it's so terribly attractive." I was having trouble talking now, but I managed, "I don't myself."

"I wanted to go to college," Larry said. "Didn't Sis ever tell you?"

I shook my head. I guess he saw it out of the corner of his eye.

"Dad had just bought the store. He and Mom had borrowed every dime they could, mortgaged everything they owned to swing it. I was going to work nights, take a few classes. No more than I could handle. We figured it would take eight or nine years."

"What the hell has this got to do with my mother?"

"It has to do with me," he said.

I would have gotten up and walked out then, if I could have, but the way we were sitting I'd have had to crawl over him.

"Then there was this politician, who was going to get me into West Point. I fell in love with that—fell in love with the whole deal, and it never happened. He couldn't swing it, he said, but I think he really gave it to somebody who could do him more good. Someday I'm going to look that somebody up and see what he did with my big chance."

"So you joined anyhow."

Larry nodded. "I thought maybe I could get into OCS. You know about the guy who wasted a village? It was in the news."

"Yeah," I said. "I remember."

"Well, I never did that." He stood up. I wasn't expecting it, and I wanted to say wait a minute, when just a minute before I'd been ready to leave myself.

"I think I'm sober enough to go home, Holly. Sober enough to drive. Don't you? Want a lift?"

I shook my head.

Larry bent over the table, whispering. "I never did that, but I would have. I got a lot of guys to fight for me, when I knew damn good and well down where I live that we weren't going to win because nobody but us wanted us to win. Some were pretty good soldiers, and quite a few of them died."

"Okay," I said. "Okay."

"I did it for me," Larry told me, "and I'd do it again. So when your mom came across, it was like I was the only sane man on earth, everybody else was crazy as a loon, and then I found one other sane person. Is that wrong?"

I looked around. There were people at a couple of tables, but they weren't paying attention to us.

Before I could open my mouth, Larry said, "It's like I was an empty house, Holly, and I've finally found somebody to live here." Then he was gone. I'd been going to say yes, it's still wrong, only I never got the chance; the way things turned out, I never did.

After that I must have spent about an hour mooching around Barton waiting for Uncle Herbert—or maybe Bugs Bunny—to tap me on the arm, only neither one of them showed. I'd never realized what a downer *Carmen* could be.

Hell, the only part I knew was the toreador song.

7

How War Came to Barton

THE next day, Saturday, was Fair Day.

I wore my rose to the Fair; and I rode with Elaine, which meant I was there way early when the first exhibitors were just beginning to unload. Everybody said what a big help I was, but half the time I hardly knew what I was doing.

When the gate opened, I took tickets and ran errands till I was ready to drop. I saw Larry and Molly, and half my teachers, and Tom and Willa Coffey, and damn near every kid in Barton; but I didn't see my father (just in case you're wondering), because he'd gone to New York a couple of days earlier; and I didn't see Uncle Herbert. But just when I was sure my legs were going to drop off, Uncle Dee saw me, and I guess he could tell how I felt from the way I looked. Anyway, he got me to relieve one of the cashiers at the Book Sale, which meant I got to sit on a folding chair, with a bridge table to lean on.

I had a great view of the main event through a window, too.

The idea was that at noon they'd hold the big drawing.

A couple of the men had nailed up a little platform, and some of the women had decorated it with big red question marks and gold coins cut out of cardboard. With the winner looking on, Larry would magic open the box, and then the winner would get it, and whatever was inside, too.

Naturally, Elaine had to make a speech first about what a lovely day it was, the blue sky and all that, and how glad she was, how glad all the ladies were, that everyone had come. She looked pretty nervous, I thought, and I didn't blame her a bit—that platform wasn't a whole lot bigger than the roof of a car, and it didn't have any railing.

Then she told all about the box, and how it probably hadn't been opened in over a hundred years, and how people in England had opened an old trunk they'd found in a bank and discovered a poem by Shelley that nobody'd known about.

Just then Aladdin Blue came by with a couple of books; they were cheap ones—I think it was only about three bucks for the two together. "Hi," I said. "I thought you were curious about Pandora's Box. You asked if I knew what was in it, remember?"

Blue nodded and looked worried. Through the window I could smell popcorn, and hear Elaine saying over the PA system, "I'm not going to pick it up and shake it for you, because it's very heavy. There's *something* in there, and if you don't believe me, you can ask the men who carried it."

I said, "Well, you can't have found out, so why aren't you out there watching?"

"I can see from here," he told me. "So can you."

"I'm here because I'm supposed to be working. Really, *have* you found out? Honest, now."

Blue shook his head.

"Then what's bugging you?"

"Do you recall the story? I've been refreshing my memory." One of the books he had was a fat, red one, and he was holding a place in it with his finger. He opened it then,

I guess to get all the names right. "Pandora was the Greek Eve," he said, "the first woman, created to punish men for accepting Prometheus' gift of fire. Aphrodite gave her beauty, Hermes persuasion, and so on and so forth; and when she was complete, they launched her like a missile at the then-wholly-male human race. Humanity had been the doing of the titan Epimetheus, and he'd set aside in a box all the qualities he felt people would be better off without—envy, malice, and so on. They gave her that box, and with it a name that meant *all-gifted*."

I told him, "It sounds like a kid's story to me."

Blue shook his head. "Why is it that people will rave all afternoon over the philosophy, the art, the literature, and the architecture of the ancient Greeks, then dismiss something like the legend of Pandora as a fairy tale?" I didn't answer, and he said, "I suppose it's because fairy tales have their own depths and hidden caverns, and dismissing one is as easy as scoffing at the other."

He laid a five on the table, but I wouldn't take it. "Hey, prove it," I said. "Show me some of those caves."

(Outside, there was a little girl in a yellow dress up on the platform with Elaine, getting her blindfold on so she could pull a ticket stub out of the big wire drum.)

"In the first place," Blue lectured, "it's a commentary on Platonism—the idea that each real thing is an imperfect attempt to duplicate an ideal one. Epimetheus had made mankind like the gods, so the gods made Pandora like a goddess. The Greeks were saying that real people are caricatures of ideal people—their gods. In the second place, think of the pure fiendishness that the Greeks attributed to those perfect gods—Pandora was human herself, and thus a part of the target as well as a part of the weapon, like the wonderful guidance mechanism that directs an ICBM, a mechanism that is vaporized when the warhead—"

"Wait a minute. This is all so interesting I'm just damned near spellbound, but what does it have to do with the box

Elaine found? Why are you so worried about it? If you think
there's really and truly such a thing as Pandora's Box, and
Elaine's got it out there on the platform with her, you're a
lot crazier than your friend the judge and my Uncle Herbert
put together. To get it to come out even, I'd have to throw
in Daffy Duck."

Blue got mad. "Of course there was a real Pandora's Box.
And of course your mother has it there on the platform with
her, just as we've got it in here, with us." Before I could
jerk my head away, he tapped my temple with the knuckles
of his free hand. "It's the part of the human brain that's
suppressed in the interests of society. You just mentioned
your uncle, and yesterday you telephoned to ask me about
him. He killed Alice Nyman Hollander because Pandora's
Box had been opened, if you like. Didn't I tell you Pandora
was also a part of the target?"

"I'm starting to think you really are crazy. You get hold
of some old story—"

Blue raised his hand to stop me. "Is that old sunshine out
there? That sun's been beating down on some part of this
planet from the beginning. In this school they no doubt teach
you that the difference between myth and history is that
history concerns past events and myth events that never
were—provided that they condescend to mention either. But
the real difference is that the events that make up history
are over and done with, while myth continues, circling our
earth forever, like the chariot of Helios."

Elaine's voice crackled from the loudspeakers again: "Five
hundred and ninety-six. Is number five hundred and ninety-
six here? You have to be present to win."

Some people in the crowd outside took it up, yelling, "Five
ninety-six!" Feeling in some dumb way that I was in a position of responsibility because Uncle Dee had handed me a
cash box, I announced, "Five ninety-six," to the assembled
browsers. "Are any of you five hundred and ninety-six? If
you are, you've won Pandora's Box."

A middle-aged guy in a Hawaiian sport shirt looked around. "That's me!"

He scooted toward the stairs, and I went over to the window and stuck my head out. "He's coming!" I yelled at Elaine. "The winner's on his way!"

"How about that," one of the other browsers said. "He was right in here with us." He had a whole stack of books, and I pushed the prices into the little calculator that went with the job and gave him a shopping bag for them. "Got to wait on cash customers," I told Blue. "Sorry, Professor."

He chuckled. "I hope you realize what a customer you lost. That was mankind. He just heard his cue, and dashed on stage to speak his lines in the five hundredth—or five hundred millionth—performance of a drama that was ancient already when some wise Greek provided it with a name."

Looking out the window, I could see the man in the Hawaiian shirt pushing through the crowd around the platform, holding his ticket over his head. I asked, "Do you really believe something bad's about to happen, Mr. Blue?"

He shook his head. "I don't *think* so. I *think* that I've been carrying on like an old woman. But I'm afraid something may, just the same—so often the old women are right. I don't suppose you know where your mother acquired that box?"

"She bought it down in Chicago someplace."

"Was there a price tag on it when you first saw it?"

"Not that I remember. What difference does it make?"

"None, I suppose. But I can tell you why I'm worried. Do you know much about the century before our own, Holly?"

"Sure, how much do you want? Abe Lincoln, the Civil War, the only good Injun's a dead Injun, Jesse James, Butch Cassidy and the Sundance Kid, Remember the Maine. . . ."

Larry was on the platform now holding a black leather case of lock tools. Somebody had taken the wire drum and the little girl down, but even so there was barely room for him and the man in the Hawaiian shirt, and Pandora's Box on its stand; Elaine was starting down the rickety steps, with Larry holding one hand to help her keep her balance.

"All right," Blue said, "that's enough, and I think you've made my point for me. It was a rough hundred years. We haven't—thank God—had a war on American soil in this century, but the Civil War was fought across half the continent. The west was lawless, and the east criminal. Indians killed whites and were killed themselves where you and I are standing now."

Out on the platform, Larry was on his knees in front of the box, monkeying with the lock.

"It was a rough era," Blue said again, "and if those people built a solid, clearly expensive chest and wrote *Pandora* on the lid, I wouldn't advise anyone to open it—and particularly not at the urging of a woman—unless he was quite confident he knew what was inside."

I guess the explosion knocked me off my feet, but really I don't remember it. I was talking with Blue, and I heard a ringing, just for a moment, like a phone or maybe an old-fashioned alarm clock. Then I was underneath a table, with books scattered all around me on the floor and my blood ruining them.

8

How I Had Breakfast in Bed
and Received Visitors

SOMEHOW I rolled out from under the table and got up. Maybe it was quiet—I don't know. My ears were ringing so bad I couldn't have heard a garage band from the front row.

I stared at the wall, because some way I'd gotten the idea it had been blown down. It hadn't, and if it had I don't think I'd have been standing there; but at the moment it seemed like a miracle to see it where it had always been.

I was all alone there in the chem lab, with so many books and so much broken glass and stinking chemicals all around that I could hardly walk. I don't suppose I would have balanced very good even if the floor had been clean. I was wearing my boots, and I could feel blood sloshing in the right one.

Just about when I got to the door, people started screaming—or maybe it was only that my ears had quieted down to where I could hear them.

Outside was a mess. Nobody had gotten there yet—no

fire trucks, no ambulances, no cops. There were people all over the ground—I thought a hundred of them were dead at least. There were others staggering around like me and half the time stepping on them. There was blood all over— some alongside people where it ought to be, and some out on the grass as if it had dropped from the sky, which maybe it had. I tripped over something and looked down, and it was a shoe, a man's brown shoe; it had laces and they were still tied, but there was no foot in it.

There were people giving first aid, and a lot more who were trying to but had forgotten anything they ever knew about it. I saw one man working over another man who looked better than he did. There were maybe a couple dozen people who were hysterical—most of them were women, but some were kids and some were men. There were dazed people wandering around for reasons they didn't under-stand, looking for something that made no sense; and after a while I realized I was one of them.

Then the sirens started. I don't know who got to the high school first, but the first thing I saw was the hook-and-ladder. There are some little trees about as tall as a good basketball player out front, and I remember having some crazy idea that the firemen would use the ladders to climb them and get bodies down. I don't know what crazy idea the firemen themselves had; maybe they just brought along their hook-and-ladder thinking it might be useful, the way you drop a pair of scissors into the basket when you're packing for a picnic.

So all of a sudden there were guys in white coats running around carrying stretchers, and firemen with stretchers and aid kits, too, only the firemen had on slickers, and those terrific hats they always have. Lots of people were finding each other: *"Bob! Oh, Bob!"* Sob, sob. *"Betty! You're okay!"* Pant, pant. *"Billy! Billy!"* *"Let go, Mom!"*

Just about then I caught sight of Aladdin Blue. Something

had happened to his shirt, and he was knotting a rag around some other guy's hand. I ran to him and grabbed him and hollered, "I thought you were dead!"

He said, "You're hurt," and bum leg and all hauled me over to an ambulance. A couple of guys there cut open my jeans and bandaged my leg, working so fast I hardly knew what they'd done. Next minute we were swaying along, going like hell and hitting every chuckhole on Main Street. Somebody'd shot me up, and I was dizzy from it. A woman on one of the other stretchers said, "Where're they taking us?" and I said, to the hospital, meaning Barton Community Hospital.

Only we never got there. We just went on and on, *"Rrrr, rrrrr, rrrrrrr . . . ,"* until I thought we had to be in Wisconsin, or maybe Canada.

I'll spare you the rest of the bloody details. There were lots of people hurt worse than I was. It turned out that B.C.H. had been full, or maybe they were saving it for the people who might really die or something, and they'd taken us to Palestine, which isn't where you think but a suburb closer to Chicago than Barton is. The emergency ward there patched me up some more—stitches and about two pints of blood this time instead of just gauze and pads—and told me I'd been cut by flying glass (which I'd already figured out for myself) and not zapped by shrapnel. That was the first time I heard of shrapnel. Then they tucked me away in one of those nice cozy hospital beds that are about five feet off the floor and eighteen inches wide, and gave me a pill, and after a while I went right to sleep.

When I woke up it was morning; and believe it or not for ten minutes or so I wasn't sure what had happened or where I was. I felt like I'd had terrible dreams all night, but whenever I tried to put a finger on them, they turned out to be something that had really happened, like my throwing my arms around Aladdin Blue and getting my blood on him. I felt, too, that somehow something had changed—that my old world had stopped while I was sitting behind the card table, and a new one had started when I came to under one of the lab tables; and I would never in my whole life ever be able to get back to my old world again. I kept telling myself it was crazy, and it's only about now that I've come to realize that it was absolutely true.

I was in a private room with nobody around to talk to me or answer questions. Instead of medicine, all I could smell was flowers; there was a big bouquet on the table beside my bed. My head hurt and my leg hurt, but I couldn't do anything about them and I wanted something that would take my mind off them. There was a TV up almost at the ceiling, looking down as you might say at me in my bed; but I didn't know how to switch it on. I kept thinking how lucky it was I'd ridden into town in the Caddy with Elaine, because if I hadn't I'd have been worried to death about Sidi, and the way it was I knew Bill would take care of him till I got back. Then I started thinking about everybody I thought might've been at the Fair and wondering if they were all right. Aladdin Blue was okay or pretty close to it, because I'd seen him. But what about Elaine? Uncle Dee? Les? Megan? Larry?

Then it hit me. What had blown up must have been Pandora's Box; and if that was right, Larry'd been right on top of it.

After about half an hour a nurse came in. She sure wasn't like the beautiful nurses you see on the tube, but she wasn't a battle-ax either, and she gave me a little smile. "We're awake! Could we see someone now? We have a visitor."

I thought it was going to be Aladdin Blue, so I said yes, but the truth was I'd have seen anybody. I also asked if there was any chance of getting some breakfast.

The nurse said she was sure there was, and a minute later a young cop I'd seen around Barton once or twice came in. Uniform, gun, the whole nine, except instead of wearing his hat he had it with his clipboard. He smiled and told me he was Officer Ritter. Blue eyes and crew-cut blond hair made him look like a handsome storm trooper. I told him I was Patient Hollander.

He sat down and laid his hat on my table and fixed up his clipboard on his knee. "I've got your name already, and your age. Where were you when it happened?"

"Why is it *you* that's asking me? Aren't you going to call in the Bomb Squad from Chicago?"

"We already have," he said, "but that's just for technical advice on the bomb."

"Who's we?"

I expected him to tighten up, but he didn't. "The Barton Police and the Pool County Sheriff's Department."

"Aren't you going to call in the FBI or something?"

He shook his head. "Only if we uncover evidence indicating that a federal law's been violated."

"Maybe I could pray in school."

"I wish you would," he said straight-faced. "I'd appreciate it. Where were you when it happened?"

So I told him just like I've told you, but in a whole lot more detail because he kept going over it and over it and asking screwy questions like how far was my table from the window, and had Blue flinched before the bomb went off. I said how could he have flinched when he didn't know there was a bomb, and he read me back all that stuff Blue had reeled off about Pandora before the explosion.

"Okay," I said, "you got me. Or anyway you got him because I shot off my mouth. But do you think he'd be dumb enough to go around talking like that if there was a bomb and he planted it?"

Straight-faced again, he said, "I don't know. Would he?"

"Heck, no. Listen, nobody's ever told me—is my mother all right? Elaine Hollander?"

He studied his clipboard. "She must be. She's not on the injured list."

"And she's not dead?"

He shook his head. "So far the only identified fatalities are Drexel K. Munroe and Lawrence L. Lief."

"So far?"

He looked grim, like it might actually be getting to him a little. "A lot of the injured are hurt worse than you are, Miss Hollander."

"I'm hip."

Just then the nurse came in with my breakfast tray: coffee, vitamin, fake orange juice, small bowl of oatmeal, table-spoon of cold scrambled eggs, and half a slice of toast. Whoopee. "I'll let you eat now," Ritter told me. "Somebody will come by to see you again later."

"Don't be a party pooper. Stay and join me."

It was too late—he was halfway to the door. The truth was I had a lot more questions to ask him; I think he must have seen them coming, and that was why he beat it. I decided next time I'd ask questions first, and if I didn't get answers I wouldn't give any.

And by golly I stuck to it, too. Next time turned out to be some kind of plainclothes detective—I never got it straight where he was from, maybe Illinois Bureau of Investigation, which is a ripoff of the FBI, exactly like it sounds. He wasn't *giving* any info and wasn't *getting* any info, and pretty soon he went away.

Lunch was peachy keen—a li'l square of broiled fish, the cutest tiny paper cup of tartar sauce, some boiled carrots, two slices of white bread, a pat of margarine, and a glass of milk. I could have cried.

After lunch came proof positive that Elaine Hollander, also known as Mommy and my Aunt Elaine, had come through with flying colors, plus talking a blue streak. "My darling, my poor little darling, you're conscious! Do you like my flowers? I was here half the night, did they tell you? How are you feeling? Isn't it just too awful, too terribly awfully terrible!"

65

"Right on," I said. Then—first things first—"You got a roll of Life Savers in that little bag? Chiclets? Breath mints? Anything?"

"No, dearest, nothing but cigarettes, and I know you're trying to stop smoking."

"Gimme a cigarette," I told her. "I'm going to eat it. As soon as you go, I'm going to eat the flowers, too." I looked at them when I said that, and all of a sudden I didn't feel funny or even hungry anymore.

"Well, you really shouldn't, you know. *I* shouldn't either. It's terribly hard on the complexion."

She lit me up. It was my first in three days, and though I've never been a heavy smoker (half a pack a day was my limit at the worst), it tasted pretty damn good. I took a big drag. "Elaine, where'd you get it?"

"Get what, dearest?" She couldn't be that dumb. She was playing for time.

"That goddamn box. By now they must have asked you fifty times already."

"*You* don't think it was the box, too, Holly dearest?" She sounded hurt. Sounding hurt's one of her very top talents, and she was so good I nearly felt sorry for her myself.

"Certainly it was in the box. It had to be in the box. Where the hell else could it have been?"

"*Anywhere* else." Elaine waved her hand so her rings made a little rainbow dazzle on the wall. "Underneath the platform, or in that man Lief's tool box. Personally, I think that man was wearing a belt of dynamite, just waiting for a chance to blow up where everyone would see him."

"*Larry Lief?*" I couldn't believe this.

"The other man—the one who won. You must have seen him raise his arms just before the bang. . . ."

"No, I didn't," I told her. I could smell her perfume over everything; over the flowers, over the smoke from our cigarettes, and the hospital smell. And somehow it was shrinking everything, bringing the bomb and the broken glass and

66

the blood and death and confusion down to the level of what-can-I-wear-for-bridge.

"Well, he did. I was watching and I saw him, and hundreds of other people must have seen him, too."

"Elaine, it had to be in the box."

She shook her head positively. "Holly, dearest, that box hadn't been opened in a great many years. If there had been a bomb in it, it would've gone off long ago. Or it wouldn't work anymore."

"I don't think they do that, Elaine. They just sit there waiting. Where'd you get it?"

"I really must be running now." She got up, smoothing her clothes. "On Wells, I believe. Or perhaps it wasn't—it was a shop I'd never been to before. Bill might know. . . .

"Holly dearest, you can't imagine what a state everything's in. All those valuable antiques, and everyone just swarming over them."

Elaine bustled out. I took a couple more drags on the butt and was grinding it to death in a little tin ashtray just as the nurse came in again. She smiled and said, "Do we think we could stand one more visitor? Our uncle's here."

9
How Blue Got the Job

I FROZE. I didn't want to say yes and I couldn't say no. The nurse smiled again, about the same way she would have at a cute knickknack. "He seems like such an interesting man, and your sister—was that your sister?—is perfectly lovely! Where does she buy her clothes?"

I stared at her, and wow did I ever feel like making some smart-ass remark; but all I could think of was here I am waiting for a crazy killer and you want to hear about Lord & Taylor.

Then Aladdin Blue came through the door. He had on slacks and an old sportcoat, which for him was most likely dressed up. What's more, he was carrying (I could hardly believe it) one of those little one-pound boxes of candy.

My brain unfroze. "Unc!" I trilled joyfully. "Uncle—"

"Al, the patient's pal. How are you doing, Holly?"

"Wonderful. It may take a miracle, but somehow—some-way—sometime—I'm determined to play the tuba again."

The nurse ducked out.

"Listen, Holly, I'm terribly sorry."

68

"What for?"

"For what I did to you—or rather, for what I failed to do. The explosion rattled me, I'm afraid. Or perhaps it was merely the shock of knowing there had been one. I didn't see you and so I didn't think about you. I went outside to help the people who'd been hurt—"

"So you didn't know I'd been cut up a little till I grabbed you and bled all over your pants."

He nodded solemnly. "I should have helped you, and did not. And now I don't know what to say, except that I am truly sorry."

I didn't know whether to laugh or cry. I said, "Pass me that candy and sit down. Then we'll talk about sorry."

I popped one in my mouth. It was an opera cream, which I love. While I was chewing it, I broke open a couple of others: caramels and nuts. *All right!*

"I ought to have known, of course," Blue said. "You were sitting in front of the window; the wall sheltered the rest of us. I didn't think—"

"How much did this cost you? About five bucks?"

He nodded.

"Small, but good stuff. You don't have much money, do you?"

"Enough for my needs."

"Well, thank you for the candy. Maybe I shouldn't eat it, but I'm going to. Listen, there were people bleeding to death out there. Screaming, too, I bet. What you did was brave. You ran—" Right there I stuck. I couldn't figure any way to suck the word back in, and I couldn't go on, and all I could see was his damned cane.

He smiled. He doesn't do it often, but you like it when he does. "Let's say I ran as fast as I could."

"You know this's really crazy?" I was chewing two caramels at once; it didn't stop me from talking, just from talking good. "Here we are, we like each other, we're not mad at each other, and we're circling around like each thinks

69

the other one's going to bite. You do like me, don't you?"

Blue nodded. "You're charming. You're also intelligent."

"And rich and jailbait, and that worries you a lot. Don't sweat it—I won't holler unless there's plenty to holler about."

"There won't be."

"I know that. Listen, if you'll open that locker, I think you'll find my jeans inside it. Will you please take your five bucks back?"

He shook his head. "Don't suggest that again."

"I didn't think you would. Why the uncle bit to bring me candy?"

"Only relatives are being admitted, so I became Alan B. Hollander. They didn't ask for identification, which is too bad because I had some. Want to see it?"

"Nope. Don't try to draw an innocent child into your evil schemes. You didn't know you were terrifying me, huh?"

"They didn't tell you my name?" Blue was looking worried again. He gets fine, close-together lines on his forehead when he's worried.

"Just that it was my uncle. You don't know about the rose, do you?"

He cocked an eyebrow at me. "I know you were wearing a paper rose in your hair when I saw you at the book sale."

So I told him all about the note from Uncle Herbert, and how I'd bought the rose and worn it ever since.

"But he hasn't contacted you?"

"Not till now." I pointed at the bouquet Elaine had bought. "See it? Down near the bottom."

He hobbled over and pulled it out—one single white rose, just starting to open. "You don't think the florist—"

"Sure I think the florist. It's a florist's rose. But I think the florist put it there because Uncle Herbert told him to, somehow. It's his way of letting me know he's around."

"It could've been part of the arrangement. Or a mistake."

"Sure it could. Hey, here I've been stuffing myself with these and never offered you any. Try one of the dark chocolate-covered pecan clusters. They're great."

"Thank you, I will," he said.

I let him take it and get back into the chair again. "I should have shown you, but I already ate it. You know what I found in here? One of those yellow marshmallow bunnies, like you get in your basket at Easter. Really."

He looked at me.

"I supposed they meant for it to be there. Or maybe it was a mistake at the factory."

I got the smile again, and this time it stayed so long he turned away so I wouldn't see it. "You win, I believe."

"Sure I do. You know as well as I do that florists don't make mistakes like that. Look at that bouquet. It's all mums and glads and greens. Bouquets are planned, and nobody would plan one that included one little white rose down at the bottom where it couldn't be seen."

"I said you win."

"Yeah."

I was quiet so long he started to stand up, but I waved a hand to let him know I wanted him to stay. "Listen, I told a lie a minute ago. I didn't mean to, but it was a lie just the same."

"A lie is an untruth stated with intent to deceive."

"Okay, it wasn't a lie—it was an untruth. I said I was rich. I should've said I come from a rich family. I actually don't have much dough—just what my father gives me for clothes. So I can't really hire you. But I want you to help me, and when I'm older I'll pay you, honest. You're a criminologist, right?"

Blue nodded.

"Well, I want you to help me find Uncle Herbert and send him back before he hurts somebody else."

"Somebody else?"

"You told me about his wife."

"Whom he killed before you were born," Blue said. "Has he harmed anyone recently, as far as you know?"

I shook my head.

"But you believe he has. Your voice betrayed you a moment ago, and your face did just now. I'll try to help, I promise—but I won't stand a chance unless we're open with each other. What is it you think he did?"

"It's obvious, isn't it? The bomb."

"You believe that he put the bomb in Pandora's Box?"

"Not in the box. I was just talking to Elaine about that, and I realized it doesn't have to have been there. Everyone was looking at the box when the bomb went off, so naturally we all think the bomb was in there. Only Elaine thinks that Munroe guy had dynamite around his waist."

I got the eyebrows again. "And do you?"

"Huh uh. He was in the book sale with us, remember? He had his shirt out of his pants, so there could have been stuff under it. But I don't think it could've been anything anywhere near as big as sticks of dynamite. I'd have seen the corners of something."

"I agree. People have done that sort of thing successfully with explosives beneath a loose-fitting overcoat, but I've never heard of hiding them under a summer shirt, and I don't think it could be done." As he spoke, Blue had been getting up to stand up. Even crippled, he got across to the door pretty quickly.

"Come in," he said. "You can hear better."

The guy who stepped into my hospital room then was as big as my father, and maybe bigger—tall and wide; quite a bit of it was probably fat, but for sure quite a bit wasn't. He had a big square face that looked like it had been hacked out of a block of wood with a machete. "By God, you're right!" he said. "But I could hear well enough out there."

Then to me: "My name's Sandoz, Miss Hollander; I'm a

county detective." He got out his badge case like he was used to doing it and flipped it open.

As primly as I could, I said, "I'm delighted to meet you, Lieutenant Sandoz. May I ask why you were spying on me?"

"Because two people are dead, Miss Hollander, and at least two more are apt to die before tomorrow morning. Whoever killed them might get a dozen next time, and next time you might be one of them. I'd do worse things than listen outside your door for a minute to stop that from happening."

Naturally I was trying as hard as I could to remember just exactly what Blue and I had said, and wondering when he'd started listening. I said, "I don't think you'll learn much from either one of us, Lieutenant Sandoz."

He smiled. It wasn't a very friendly smile, only a little twitch of his wooden lips, but I think it was probably about as friendly as he could make it. "I'll be the judge of that, Miss Hollander. I've already learned, for example, that someone you call Elaine—that will be Elaine Calvat Hollander, your mother, I suppose—thinks Munroe had a bomb on him. Now when I see her I'll have something else to talk about."

"Do *you* think so?" Blue wanted to know. He crossed to the chair and sat down again.

"I don't know enough yet to have an opinion. Can I ask who you are, sir?"

"My name's Aladdin Blue," Blue said. So much for my uncle Al.

"And what are you doing here?"

"That should be obvious. I'm visiting Miss Hollander."

I said, "He brought me some candy," and held out the box. "Want a piece, Lieutenant Sandoz?"

I got ignored. "I'm afraid you'll have to go now, sir."

There was no mincing around with Blue; he just shook his head. "I won't."

"I'm afraid you'll have to."

"If you speak to the hospital authorities, and argue with them long enough, I'm certain they'll order me to leave," Blue said. "But before you do, I think you should consider whether you really want to."

"I've considered it," Sandoz told him. "Get out."

Blue made a toy steeple of his fingers. "I am a Hollander employee," he said "As you must know by now, Mr. Hollander is in New York on business. I spoke with him by telephone before coming here, and although he is unable to return, he is deeply concerned about his daughter's welfare, and—"

"The planes don't fly out of New York on Sunday? They sure land at O'Hare."

"Mr. Hollander is involved in negotiations that will affect the future of the corporation profoundly," Blue said. "Such negotiations are not suspended on Friday afternoon and resumed on Monday morning; but even so, he may drop everything and come. I had hoped, when I left here, to be able to tell him that would not be necessary. Meanwhile I am here *in loco parentis*. Miss Hollander is a minor; she has suffered serious injuries and loss of blood. We're in Cook County, so you aren't even in your own jurisdiction. I don't think you're so stupid as to try to eject me, a cripple, by force under those circumstances. But if you are, I assure you I will file suit against you and Pool County tomorrow."

"You pointed out yourself," Sandoz said, "that I could get one of the doctors here to put you out. What would you do then—sue the hospital because your visiting time was up? Why make it tough for me? I've got nothing against you now. Why give me something?"

"I'm trying not to," Blue said. "In fact, I'm trying to help you. Suppose Miss Hollander's condition worsens tonight? Not because of anything you said or did—conditions sometimes do. I'll have to tell Mr. Hollander that I was here and you forced me to leave so that you could cross-examine his

74

daughter. Have you thought about how that might look, how it might sound? How will you defend yourself—by proving that Miss Hollander's an insane explosives expert?"

(Blue was watching Sandoz's face when he said that and so was I, because I knew right away that he was trying to see if Sandoz had been listening when I'd said Uncle Herbert might be the one. Maybe it looked to Blue like Sandoz's nose lit up and his eyes went around, but it sure didn't to me. I might as well have been watching a wooden Indian.)

"That's nonsense and you know it," Blue went on. "You're far better off with Munroe's dynamite. Now if you want to fetch a resident or the chief nurse, go ahead. When I'm gone, you can quiz Miss Hollander to your heart's content. But I'd be careful, if I were you, not to say anything that might offend her. It's quite possible she might become hysterical. You know how girls her age are."

10
How Sandoz Dropped
the Bomb on Us

I SAID, "I don't care if Mr. Blue stays or goes. I'll probably have more fun with him not around."

Naturally that did it—Sandoz figured I was laying for him. He growled, "You can stay," at Blue and went off to find another chair.

When he came back with one and had gotten himself settled, he gave me this little speech about how there was really nothing serious he wanted to ask me—just routine—and it would all be over in ten minutes. I felt like saying I thought the routine stuff was what they'd sent Ritter, my handsome storm trooper, to get. Only I decided that Blue and I'd already pushed him plenty far enough, so I made my eyes get wide and my face go innocent and nodded a lot while I nibbled another chocolate. Of course I thought he'd start on Pandora's Box. Wrong.

He put on a little show of flipping through a notepad he took out of his breast pocket. Then he said, "As I understand it, you were a friend of Drexel K. Munroe."

"You're nuts."

"That was the information we received. Are you saying you didn't know Munroe?"

"Who told you I knew him?"

"I'm afraid I have to keep that confidential. Mr. Munroe had a daughter about your age. Her name's Tracy."

I shook my head, which hurt. "I don't know any Tracies."

"She goes to your school."

"Do you know how many kids go to Barton High? There are lots of colleges with smaller enrollments."

He smiled. I was getting so used to that wooden puss I could tell now when the lips moved. "There must be a lot of them you don't know."

"If I haven't had a class with them and they're not in the riding club or the rifle club, it's twenty to one I don't know them."

"Or if they're not the children of your parents' friends, I suppose. You'd know them, I imagine."

Before I could think, I said, "My parents don't have any friends." It was out of my mouth before I realized I'd never thought of it before, but it was true.

"Really?" Sandoz cocked his head to look at me, just the tiniest little bit.

Blue said, "Mr. and Mrs. Hollander are widely acquainted."

"You butt out, or I'll call that doctor and have you take a walk after all."

I tried to fix it. "What I mean is they don't have friends *together*. My father's are mostly business people. My mother's are ladies she's met in various clubs she belongs to—women from around here."

"Which were the Munroes?"

"Neither one, as far as I know. Why don't you ask Elaine?"

Sandoz turned to Blue. "You say the Hollanders are

widely acquainted. Did they know Mr. and Mrs. Munroe?"

Blue shrugged. "They might well have, but to the best of my knowledge they did not."

"Okay." Back to me. "What about this guy Lief?"

"What about him?"

"You know him?"

"Naturally I knew him. He was my best friend's brother."

"But your mother didn't know him?"

(Watch it!) "Sure she knew him. She was the one who fixed it for him to open the box. Everybody you've talked to must've told you that. Everybody knew it—she was in charge. You think she had something against him and set this whole thing up to do him in? Nuts again."

"You said that, Miss Hollander. Not me. Did your father know him?"

"Sure."

"Although he and Mrs. Hollander have no friends in common?"

"That's not what I meant. He wasn't that kind of friend."

Blue asked, "Are you working on the theory that the deaths of Munroe and Lief were planned in some way? In other words, that the bomb was intended to kill those two men specifically?"

"We consider that one possibility."

"That interests me. I would have thought it obvious that they were simply the people who happened to be closest to the explosion. Unless you're back to Munroe's dynamite belt again."

Sandoz scratched his cheek with a thick forefinger. "Some guy gets run down in traffic. Would you figure he just happened to be standing in front of somebody's bumper at the wrong time? That would make a car a hell of a lot better weapon than a gun—it is anyhow in my book, but if we thought like that it would be better yet. No, when we find some poor bastard flattened on the pavement, we kind of

78

routinely ask if somebody wanted him dead. Pretty often the answer is yes."

"And you think someone wanted Munroe and Lief dead," Blue said.

"No, I don't think so. I'm just willing to consider it."

Before I could shut my mouth I said, "The little kid!"

"Yes, Miss Hollander?"

"The little girl. She was up on the platform blindfolded. She pulled out the ticket."

Sandoz nodded, and for just a minute there he looked like he might be somebody's grandfather. "Her name's Nancy Noonan. A sweet child, I'm told. I haven't talked to her yet."

"But if somebody wanted Mr. Munroe killed, they'd have had to arrange for him to win."

"That's a good point," Sandoz said. "In fact, I'd call it an excellent point. In my opinion it wouldn't have been utterly impossible for somebody to do that, however."

"You're putting me on."

"No, not really, Miss Hollander. I used to work the bunco squad, and a lot of what we did concerned crooked gambling. You wouldn't know about that, I'm sure, but you'd be surprised just how easy it is to fix a game that looks like it's on the up-and-up. Take that drawing. You and Mr. Blue here both saw it, from what I've heard. How was it done, Mr. Blue?"

Blue shook his head, his lips tight. I said, "They put all the tickets in a big wire drum—my mother borrowed it from some church. They cranked it around, and the little girl pulled out the winning ticket."

"Not quite, Miss Hollander. A couple of our officers have already talked to several witnesses. Shall I tell you how it was really done?"

Naturally I nodded. I knew damned well he was setting me up, but there wasn't anything else to do.

"You said that 'they' cranked the drum. It was Mrs. Elaine Hollander who cranked it. Then little Nancy, blindfolded, took out a ticket. She gave it to Mrs. Hollander, and Mrs. Hollander announced the number—five ninety-six."

"There was no way she could have known what the number on that ticket would be."

Sandoz got a cigar out of his shirt pocket, peeled off the plastic, and rubbed it between his hands. If it had been one of those see-how-smart-I-am numbers, it wouldn't have bothered me, or anyway I don't think it would. Only it wasn't. He was just sitting there with that blank brown face, rolling a new stogie between mitts that looked like they could crack coconuts.

Then he said, "Why would she have to know the number of the ticket? Say she wanted five ninety-six to win. All she'd have to do would be to look at the ticket—whatever number it was—and call out five ninety-six. Who'd know the difference? The little girl? She was blindfolded. After the number was called, the ticket would go back into the barrel."

I stopped chewing while he lit up. He looked like a guy who'd carry kitchen matches, but it was an old beat-up Zippo, the kind that works forever.

"Those folks watching weren't gamblers," he said, "and your mother's a prominent woman there in Barton. Nobody'd accuse her of cheating. Nobody has."

"You just did."

"No, Miss Hollander, I didn't. I told you it wouldn't have been utterly impossible to get Munroe up on that platform. You didn't believe me, so I gave you an instance."

"Elaine couldn't have known what his ticket number was," I said.

Sandoz shook his head, "Hypothetically I could give you three ways, easy."

"Okay, give them! I still won't believe you."

Sandoz looked from me to Blue as if he was waiting for Blue to object. When he didn't, Sandoz said, "In the first place, we asked about those tickets. There were two gates where people could get in, and there were rolls of tickets at each gate. The tickets on each roll were numbered sequentially. Suppose that somebody—anybody—was hanging around there and spotted Munroe in line. Say there were nine ahead of him and this somebody saw that the person being sold a ticket right then had five eighty-seven. That's one.

"Or suppose that this somebody had herself a badge and a ribbon. She goes up to him and says, 'Pardon me, sir, but do you have a ticket?' What would he do—holler that he'd never been so insulted in his life? I don't think so. I wouldn't have, if it was me. I'd have just pulled out my stub, the stub I was saving because I knew there'd be a drawing, and shown it to her. I think most people would. That's two.

"Or she could just ask him. Why not? That's three."

"Because it would be dumb," I told him. "That's why not. Elaine was in charge of everything, and in charge of the drawing especially. And it would have looked as fishy as hell for her to go around asking people what their numbers were."

"I wasn't talking about your mother," Sandoz said. "I was just talking about somebody who wanted to find out. But if this somebody were involved with the drawing some way, she could have somebody else do it for her. A kid, maybe. After all, they got a little girl to pull out the winning ticket, and that's because people tend to trust little girls."

"She's my mother. God knows I'm not crazy about her, and you've probably found that out. But do you think that if she . . . I'd . . ."

For a minute I could have sworn that wooden face looked unhappy. "No," he said. "No, I don't."

Softly, Blue told me, "He wanted to watch your expression."

It took me a while to get it. Then I said, "Well, he saw it."

Sandoz was looking at Blue. "You a lawyer?"

Blue shook his head.

"Well, you look like one. What are you?"

"I'm a criminologist."

"I thought you said you worked for the father."

"Didn't it ever strike you that a company that manufactures safes and locks might make good use of a criminologist? I said I was a Hollander employee, I think. I am."

"Did *you* know Munroe?"

Blue shook his head again.

"How about Lief?"

"Yes. I knew Lief."

"Everybody knew Lief, it seems like. Only not together. Did you meet him through Mr. Hollander or Mrs. Hollander?"

"No."

"See, I told you. How did you meet him?"

"That's my affair."

"You're not going to cooperate with the police?"

"Not to the point of divulging my personal affairs when they are not germane."

Sandoz turned back to me. "What about you, Miss Hollander? You said you knew him because he was your best friend's brother, which is entirely reasonable; but you said that your father knew him, too. Are you willing to tell me what the connection between them was?"

"Sure," I said. "Locks."

"Locks?"

"It's obvious, isn't it? Locks are my father's business, and his hobby, too. Larry was a locksmith. He sold some of the products our company makes, and he was about the only person in town my father could talk to about tumblers and false wards and double-key systems and all that junk."

"How about your mother?"

"My mother knew him because he came to the house sometimes to drop off Megan, or to pick her up."

"Through you, in other words."

"That's right. Through me."

"Judging from the pictures I've seen he was a good-looking man. She like him?"

"No." I shook my head, thinking that Elaine never really liked anybody except Elaine. Then all of a sudden I remembered what the bomb must have knocked out of me, and I told Sandoz all about coming to see Megan at the Magic Key shop, and what Molly had said, and about the car and so on. Only for Molly's sake I left out her gun.

This time his smile was practically real. "You should've given us that sooner," he told me.

"I know." I felt humble. "Only I didn't think of it. I wasn't thinking that the bomb might have been aimed—you know what I mean—at Larry. You were the one who started me doing that."

It looked like Sandoz was going to smile again, but he got it under control. He stood up, brushing the cigar ashes off his legs. "I'll be going now," he said. "I think I'll have a talk with Mrs. Lief. I may be seeing you again later, Miss Hollander. And you, Mr. Blue."

Blue raised his cane to stop him. "Before you leave, I'd like to ask you one question. It will influence the report I make to Mr. Hollander a great deal, I think."

"Go ahead and ask," Sandoz told him. "I don't promise to answer and I don't care what you tell your boss, but there's no harm in asking."

"You indicated obliquely that you suspected Mrs. Hollander. I know you said nothing actionable, and you may not even have been serious. But whether you were serious or not, do you have any real evidence to show that the bomb was in that box?"

Sandoz pushed the cane to one side. "I have evidence that shows that it wasn't, Mr. Blue," he said. "That it wasn't even a bomb."

He went out the door.

11

How Blue Helped Me Figure
Things Out

I TOOK a deep breath, maybe two or three. Then I said,
"Well, that's over with."

Blue shrugged. "I hope so."

"Did you really call my father in New York? That was
nice of you."

"I was angling for a job. I still am, because I need the
money. Anyway, everything I told Lieutenant Sandoz was
true. A safe and lock company should have a criminologist
on its staff, or at least have a criminological consultant to
call in at need. I am a Hollander employee—you're a Hollander, and you've asked me to help you and offered to pay
me. I accept."

"What did he say?"

"Your father? He was concerned about you and your
mother. Your mother had called him at his hotel last night,
and he had watched a morning news show—"

"My God, you're right! We must've been on TV. How
do you turn that thing on?"

Blue looked as though he was disappointed in me, which I suppose he had a right to. "There won't be anything now until six. You've got plenty of time."

"Just the same, I want to know."

We hunted around and finally found a remote that had fallen down behind the table. When I had tested it out, I asked Blue again about my father.

"He wanted to know if I had seen your mother; he was afraid she had been concealing something when she had assured him that she was not injured. I told him I had not, but that she wasn't hospitalized. We talked for some time about the extent of your injuries. I'm certain he's spoken with your doctor by now. He expressed the opinion that the bombing—that, at least, was what we called it—had been the act of radical terrorists. I believe that was all."

"How did you know where to call him, anyway?"

"I telephoned your housekeeper and inquired. He had wisely left the name of his hotel with her in case of emergencies, and I was able to catch him in his room this morning before he left for his meeting."

"I'm surprised Mrs. Maas gave it to you."

"I think she did so under the impression that I was calling in an official capacity, although I did not say I was."

"What a shock when she thought so, I'll bet. I wonder how she ever got a wild idea like that! You're pretty slick, aren't you?"

Blue shook his head. "I used to think I was, but I've been disabused of that idea. I know a few tricks, and occasionally I invent a new one. That's all. With the right backdrop and the right lighting, I can fool most of the audience on a good night. Not without them, and not all the audience—not ever."

"Modest, too."

"Are you in much pain?"

"A little. I guess being so hungry took my mind off it, or

85

maybe they gave me some kind of dope and it's getting weaker now. I imagine I'll be going around like you, with a cane, for a while."

As soon as I was finished, I was sorry. I could see the hurt in his eyes. He said, "You are wondering whether my own trouble is permanent or temporary. It is permanent."

"How'd it happen?"

"That doesn't matter now."

He was getting set to stand up, so I yelled at him. "Hey, don't go, I promise not to talk about it anymore. I thought you wouldn't mind, since I've paid dues myself." All the time I was feeling around inside my head for something that would keep him where he was and not make him mad. "Where do you live?"

He stopped pushing on the handle of his stick. "In South Barton. I own an old farmhouse."

"A farm, huh? That's nice."

"Most of the land has been sold off, but there are still a few acres of woods left. The house was built during the Civil War, and I suppose nine out of ten people who see it think it abandoned."

I said, "I'd like to come by and take a look, when I'm up and around again. Listen, I'm not keeping you from anything, am I? It's just that I like your company."

"You're afraid of your uncle. That's very understandable, but I'll have to go soon."

Those blue Blue eyes could see right through me; that was scarier, almost, than thinking about Uncle Herbert.

Blue continued, "If it's of any comfort to you, I think you tend to exaggerate the threat posed by your uncle. As I've told you before, psychotics rarely harm anyone except themselves; and from what the judge has passed along to me, it's been ten years or more since Herbert Hollander posed a problem to the staff at Garden Meadow."

"Going over the wall isn't a problem?"

"It certainly doesn't indicate a propensity for violence."

"Let's change the subject. Do you know Megan Lief? Was she hurt? Nobody'll tell me."

"I don't believe so," Blue said. He reeled off the names of the other casualties. I didn't recognize any of them.

I said, "I sort of expected that Uncle Dee would come up to see me."

"I didn't know you had another uncle."

"Not a real uncle. Uncle Dee is De Witte Sinclair—do you know him?"

Blue was smiling. "I've scouted books for him a few times."

"Scouted?"

"A book scout is to a rare-book dealer what a jackal is to a tiger. He buys books cheaply and sells them to the dealer for what they're worth. Then the dealer locates a customer willing to pay a great deal more than they're worth, and resells them to him. That, at least, is the way we book scouts tell it. Have you considered that if De Witte tried to see you they wouldn't let him come up? At least, not unless he told the kind of fib I did."

That made me feel better. "No," I said, "I hadn't thought of that. Maybe he came after all, huh? But you know, I'll bet he's too busy trying to straighten up the book sale— that would be just like him. What do you suppose they'll do with all those books now?"

"I have no idea."

"Save them for next year, I guess—if there's a Fair next year at all. Do you think it was those guys who were bothering Larry?"

Blue shook his head.

"Why not? That Lieutenant Sandoz did. Don't you think he's a good cop?"

"Yes," Blue answered slowly. "Yes, I think he's a good cop."

"You're holding something back." (Sometimes I'm damned insightful myself.)

Blue said, "Holly, you have to understand that, at least in nine cases out of ten, the police are not actually interested in arresting the guilty party. Under the law, the determination of guilt isn't even their responsibility. What they want and need is someone who can plausibly be brought before a judge. A good cop—and I agree, I think Sandoz is probably one—still has that urge, sometimes at least, to discover what really happened. But even a good cop cannot help being influenced by his training and pressure exerted by his superiors."

"So the people who were phoning Larry could just be babies to throw to the wolves? How do you know?"

"You heard me tell Sandoz that I knew him. That was how I came to meet him. A mutual friend suggested I might be able to help him."

"Who were they? Did he give you their names?"

"I think he knew more than he told me. But I learned that they objected—if that is the word—to something he had done in Vietnam. When Larry applied for a loan to set up his business, they had sent an anonymous letter to one of the officers of the bank, accusing Lief of unspecified crimes against humanity. If their objective was to sour the loan, as I suppose it was, they failed. I would not imagine that an unsigned letter would have much effect on a bank unless its accusations concerned financial malfeasance. The officers are not generally the sort of men who view crimes against humanity with severity. I spent some time trying to locate that letter—it was the only tangible clue in sight—but it had been destroyed. Then this happened."

"In other words, they got him." My leg was hurting pretty bad by then, and I was feeling sorry for myself.

"I doubt it. That's why I didn't tell my little story to Lieutenant Sandoz."

"Maybe you doubt it, but nobody else would."

Blue stood up, looking grim. "Then isn't that all the more reason for me to do what I can to keep the investigation on the right path? What are war crimes? Torturing prisoners, perhaps, or multiplying civilian deaths. Professional dissidents might use those accusations to extenuate any actions of their own, and in fact apologists for the American policy in Vietnam used the very real war crimes of the North Vietnamese to excuse ours. But these people appeared to be anything but professional; they struck me as conscience-stricken blunderers. They might, just conceivably, have been carried to the point of destroying the object of their hatred. But would they do that by detonating an infernal device that not only might, but actually did, kill or mutilate a dozen blameless people? I suppose you're too young to remember the comic strip *Pogo,* but there was a character called Deacon Mushrat who urged the others to *'Kill the warmongers! Bomb them off the face of the earth!'* That was a comic-strip pacifist, however."

"But Larry's dead, so it could have been them. Only you don't think it was. Who do you think?"

"I don't think. I need more facts." He had gone over to the window, and was looking out. It wasn't dark yet—in fact it was only the middle of the afternoon—but I had the feeling that for him it was night out, that he was staring into blackness.

I said, "Sandoz sounded like he thought it might be Elaine. Did you buy that?"

"No." Blue turned to face me. "Did you?"

"Maybe a little."

"Why?"

"Oh, just because he made it sound so good. Fixing the drawing, finding out what ticket Munroe had. All that."

"Yes, it was beautifully logical. However, you followed it to the place Sandoz wanted you to go, and not to the place where it had led Sandoz. I'm still not quite certain why, but Sandoz wanted you to believe he might accuse your mother. What all of that really meant was that unless Mrs. Hollander was the killer, Munroe was not the target.

Anyone might have learned his ticket number, just as Sandoz said. But only your mother could have arranged for that number to be the winner. Besides, if someone had merely wanted to kill Munroe, and wasn't concerned about the possible deaths of others, why not put a bomb in his car in the parking lot? The Mob does such things all the time. Why bother with so much folderol?"

I had been thinking, a bad habit my teachers hadn't quite knocked out of me. "Wait a minute! There's another way someone could've fixed the numbers. Suppose it was somebody that little girl— What was her name? Nancy Noonan? Suppose it was somebody Nancy trusted, and somehow he got hold of Munroe's ticket. I took tickets for a while, and I was just dropping them into a box. He could have pretended he had to tie his shoe or scratch his ankle, or if it was a woman maybe pull up a heel strap, just after Munroe went in. Later, he'd give the ticket to Nancy and tell her they were going play a joke or something, and she was only supposed to pretend to reach into the drum."

Blue said, "He could never rely on a child that age to keep his secret."

"Maybe he figured she'd be killed too when the bomb went off—only Sandoz says it wasn't a bomb. Well, whatever it was. He probably thought Munroe'd be right there in the crowd watching the drawing instead of inside at the book sale with us. If he'd been outside, there wouldn't have been time for her to get down off the platform. Anyway, the murderer would think that even if he missed her, he could—"

I broke off because all of a sudden the chocolate in my stomach had turned to vinegar ice. Besides, there wasn't any use in going on with it. Blue's face doesn't give away much, but it's nowhere near as expressionless as Sandoz's, and I was learning to read it; it was blank now, just no expression at all, and that meant he had pulled into himself and was thinking so hard that he didn't have any attention to spare for it. "She should be under guard," he said. "And of course the police must speak with her as soon as possible. When it becomes known that they have, she'll be out of danger." He checked out my bedside table. "I must find a telephone."

That was when a nurse I hadn't seen before came bustling in. "There are public telephones in an alcove off the lobby, sir. The receptionist can show you, but you'll have to go now. Visiting hours are over."

Then to me: "Have you heard about the murder?" Her eyes were shining. What a treat!

"It wasn't a little girl. . . ."

"Oh, no. An old man. They found him by the parking lot, right here at our hospital!"

She bustled out again, this time with Blue after her like a lame hound that can still run when a bunny jumps under its nose. I head the thump of his cane out in the corridor, and then the murmur of their voices; the only words I could make out, though, were what he said last: "I'd better go down and talk to them. I think I may be able to identify him."

12
How I Heard Some News

AFTER dinner when the news came on, I was right there waiting. One good thing about living close to a big city like Chicago is that you get a full hour of local stories from a station that can spring for mobile units and good reporters. My favorite's Ben Jacobs, a good-looking Jew about thirty-five or forty who doesn't care what the hell he says or who the hell he says it to, and gets fighting mad about at least half the stories they cover. Naturally I was hoping tonight was my big night with Ben—if I couldn't be in his arms, at least I'd be on his lips. But when they finally got around to "the Barton Bombing," it was Gerri Corkeran. Gerri's a pretty lady with big eyes and hair like a gold helmet, but she isn't Ben Jacobs.

Besides, as soon as she started I realized I was really a day too late. All the big, exciting coverage had been the night before, when I was out of it. What Gerri had was follow-up. She interviewed Mrs. Munroe, who turned out to have one of those pushed-together faces and a couple little kids, besides a dumb-looking daughter about my age.

And then, so help me, there were Molly and Megan and old Mr. Lief from the shoe store, all sitting side-by-each on the living-room sofa.

    Gerri: "I might as well ask the inevitable question and get it over. How does it feel to have your son survive two tours in Vietnam, and then have him die like this?"

(Mr. Lief doesn't answer—just shakes his head. He has one of those bent-down pipes in his mouth, but it doesn't seem to be lit.)

    Molly: "It was them! I know it was."

(Megan nudges her, but she won't shut up.)

    Gerri: "It was who, Mrs. Lief?"

    Molly: "The ones that used to phone. They haven't called no more. Not since Larry passed on, not one call. They got him, but I'm goin' to get them."

    Megan: "It didn't have to be them. Everybody knows Larry's dead now."

    Gerri: "Your husband was receiving threatening calls, Mrs. Lief?"

    Molly: "Yes!" *(Cries.)*

    Megan: "No!"

    Gerri: "Do you know anything about this, Mr. Lief? Have you informed the police?"

    Lief: "I personally only answered one crank call, and that was at least six months back. I'd practically forgotten about them. They weren't actually threatening—at least the one I answered wasn't."

    Megan: "The police know already. They've talked to us."

(Back to the studio, where Gerri's sitting at one of those long lunch-counter desks TV newspersons use and nobody else does.)

    Ben: "Gerri, what were those calls about?"

    Gerri: "It took a lot of digging—Mrs. Lief was very upset, and Lawrence Lief's father and sister didn't want to talk, but whoever called told war stories, if I can put it that way."

Ben: "War stories?"

Gerri: "Yes, from Vietnam. All this may've had nothing to do with the bombing."

Ben: "But it might. Did it really end months ago, as the victim's father implied?"

Gerri: *(Shaking her head.)* "Ben, the victim's wife received one two days ago—the day before he was killed."

Then off they went to look at a million white chickens that had gotten loose on the Dan Ryan Expressway. If I'd had Les or somebody there to talk to, I'd have bitched because Megan never mentioned my name or said I'd been hurt; but what I was really thinking about mostly were Munroe's kids, kids that weren't nice-looking or anything, and now no daddy.

Then I started wondering whether Megan knew it was me who told the cops about the calls, and if she did, whether she was mad. If she didn't, sooner or later I was going to have to tell her. It wasn't Larry that I felt sorry for, or Munroe either. Munroe had just been a guy in a loud shirt, like a million other guys; Larry's troubles were over. I felt sorry for Munroe's dim little wife and her three kids, whose troubles had just begun. And for Megan and Molly and Larry's dad. Especially for old Mr. Lief, because although he wasn't showing it, I had the feeling he was the one who'd never get over it.

Baseball then. You can't get away from baseball scores on the news. The Cubs lost. The Sox lost. Watching the TV news, you'd think there isn't one pitcher in baseball who can throw a strike. Every time they show somebody at the plate, you can bet he's going to get wood on the ball, even if he's thrown out at first, maybe. If I were managing the Cubs, I'd have a hundred curvy cheerleaders, like the Honeybears or the Dallas Cowgirls; and when a guy from the other team was at bat and they revved up the TV cameras for him to sock one, I'd signal my Cutecubs to shake their goodies to get his eye off the ball. All the other teams would have to sign gay players, and it would change the entire complexion of the game.

When we'd seen the run that beat the Cubs and the run that beat the Sox (there's a joke there, but I wouldn't want you to think I go after every one I see), the newsroom was back, with Cutter Williams, anchorman supreme, in one of his five-hundred-dollar suits. "Our city has been the site of many famous crimes and the home of many famous criminals. John Gacy lived here; so did Al Capone. But for each famous crime we remember, there are hundreds of others we forget. That, tonight, is the subject of Ben's Commentary."

Ben was always away from the lunch counter for this, turned around in a swivel chair, at a messy desk that might really have been his. "There was a terrible explosion in Barton yesterday," he said. His face wasn't Sad the way an actor's face gets; just serious. "Today's papers are full of it, and the televised news shows—such as this one—are full of it. Even the politicians are full of it, at least when we reporters are asking questions. It's always safe, politically, to be against a mad bomber.

"Two men were killed in Barton, other people were hurt—"

Hey, that's me! Lookit me, Ben!

"And many more might have been killed. But in the thirty hours or so since the Barton bombing, eight other persons have been killed on the streets and in the homes and bars of Greater Chicago. A famous poet, T.S. Eliot, once wrote, 'This is the way the world ends, not with a bang but a whimper.' Those eight have hardly had the whimper, as far as the politicians and the news are concerned. We talk about a war against crime. They're the casualties of the skirmishes of the war crime fights against us. Just before we went on the air tonight we got word that the body of an elderly man, as yet unidentified, had been found near a parking area in the northwestern suburb of Palestine. He had been shot in the chest with a thirty-eight, and his pockets were empty except for sixty-two cents in change and a torn artificial rose. Just like one of those poppies they sell on the street for the casualties in the VA hospitals—casualties that nobody remembers."

Then Ben was gone and we were left with a couple California beach bums peddling beer. I started to yell and pound the damn whiter-than-white scratchy sheet, and after a while I remembered to turn off the TV and yell louder. It wasn't very long before a nurse came running to ask what was the matter, and pretty soon an orderly came too and held my arms down until I shut up.

"I know him," I said when they finally got me quieted down. "It's got to be him. I want to see him." And I told them all about it, just the way I've been telling you, only not quite so organized. And naturally they didn't call the police or Aladdin Blue, or even my father in New York. They just made me swallow some kind of pill that had me out like a Cubbie in ten minutes.

When I woke up there was sunshine coming in the window. I had a visitor, too, but she didn't look at all like the one I'd had the morning before, even aside from being a woman. She was little, with a big nose and frizzy hair and bright black eyes. Like the other one she had on a uniform, but hers was the white medical kind. When she saw my eyes were open, she said, "Hello. How are you feeling?"

Which was a switch. The nurses always said, "How are *we* feeling?"

"I feel great," I told her. "When do I get out of here?"

"This afternoon, perhaps. It will be up to your doctor, and he'll see you then. However, that doesn't mean you'll be able to stand on that leg."

"Is someone coming for me?"

96

"I don't know," she said. "Do you think there's a chance no one will?"

I noticed then that she had a clipboard in her lap, and she was holding a pen. Her fingers made just a little twitch with the pen, as if she had written, maybe, half a word. I said, "I guess they'll have to send somebody. Maybe Bill."

"Who is Bill?"

"Who are you?" I asked. "That's what I want to know."

"I'm Dr. Rothschild, and I'm a psychiatric intern here. You can call me Ruth."

"So they're afraid I'm crazy."

Dr. Rothschild shook her head. "We're afraid you may be emotionally shaken. After what you went through it would hardly be surprising."

"Aren't I supposed to be lying on a couch?"

"Not for me. I'm not a Freudian. Do you remember last night, when you began to scream?"

By then I was smarter; I didn't try to tell her everything. I just said, "I was watching the news, and they had a story on it about finding an unidentified man dead. It was my uncle, and I started to cry."

"You're sure this man was your uncle? How did you know, Holly?" (My name was on the chart thing at the foot of my bed, naturally.)

"Because of something he had in his pocket. They told about it on TV. It was my Uncle Herbert."

"What did he have?"

"You're not going to believe this," I said, and I was sure she wasn't.

"Try me."

"A fake rose."

"And that made you certain the man was your uncle?" The pen twitched on the clipboard again.

I tried to put it together for her in a way she'd believe. "In the first place, they didn't find him just anywhere; he was found here, I think, near the parking lot of this hospital—one of the nurses came in last night and said a dead man had been found there; and later it was on TV, and they said it had been in Palestine, which it would be if it was here. He was coming to see me, I think. A rose was, well, a sort of secret signal between him and me."

Dr. Rothschild smiled. She wasn't pretty, but when she smiled that way she was beautiful. "I used to have a signal like that with my grandmother," she said. "I'd wear a comb in my hair, and it meant that there was trouble at home, and she should stay or take me with her if she had to go. Usually it was Mother and Father fighting." She stopped smiling. "So I understand. I'm sorry that your uncle's dead, if it was your uncle."

"You loved your grandmother," I said. "I don't want to fool you; I didn't love my uncle."

"Perhaps he loved you."

"Yeah, maybe he did. I was scared of him, but you don't want to hear about that. Would you do me a favor? It would make me feel a lot better, and that's what you're supposed to do, right? Call up the police, or wherever they have his body. Ask if he's been identified, and if he hasn't, tell them he's Herbert Hollander. Say I can identify him when I get there, or if they'll send a picture."

Dr. Rothschild went out and came back in about five minutes with a white phone that plugged into a jack in the wall, and a phone book. It took some calling around before she reached the right party, then she said who she was and that she was calling for a patient who might be a member of the family. She put me on, and I said, "Hello, this is Holly Hollander."

"Detective Corning. Wait a minute." I could hear papers rattle. "You're the man's niece?" (He didn't say *dead man's*.)

"Yes. How'd you know?"

"A guy identified him last night. He said he had a brother named George Henry Hollander, and a niece. You don't sound like George Henry."

"That would have been Aladdin Blue."

"That's the name. Listen, Miss Hollander, you wouldn't know where he picked up a paper rose, would you?"

I said I didn't have any idea, but that you could buy them in novelty shops.

"Sure. Listen, your uncle was, ah . . ."

"Emotionally shaken or something. I think that's what they say." I gave Doc Rothschild a look.

"Right. Miss Hollander, we traced him back to the place he got loose from—"

(Sure you did. Aladdin Blue told you.)

"That was probably why he didn't have a watch or a wallet on him, or much money. Sometimes a mugger gets sore when the victim doesn't have a lot of money, and that might've been why he was shot. Just the same, we wondered about the rose."

"It's not against the law to have a phony rose, is it? I used to have one myself."

There was a long pause. Then Detective Corning said, "The thing is that it was in his side jacket pocket. He was shot in the chest. The bullet stayed in him, and it stopped his heart right away, so there wasn't a lot of bleeding. But this rose we got out of his pocket's got bloodstains on it. Would you know anything about that, Miss Hollander?"

13
How Me and Blue Deduced

MAYBE I ought to skip over leaving the hospital, but I'll just hit it lightly. Except for my father, who wasn't back from New York yet, the whole damn household came to get me. I couldn't believe it. Bill pushed my wheelchair and lifted me into the backseat of the Caddy, Mrs. Maas fussed, and Elaine yelled and bossed. I never felt so important in my life.

What's more, I don't think I was ever so glad to see anyplace as I was to see my own funky little bedroom on the second floor. It was small, sure, and messy, you bet. The TV wouldn't turn on and off or change channels unless I got out of bed and hopped over with my crutch. But that was probably good therapy for me, and there was my own phone beside my bed, and my own books and records and stuff. Heaven! It turned out Mrs. Maas had saved the paper for me—I may well be the nation's leading *Doonesbury* fanatic—so I got to read all about it and find my own name on the injured list. Then, just when I'd finished that and the funnies and the lady who gives smart-ass advice, and had read all about the President and a couple of good fires, and was settling down to recipes and big-city politics, Mrs. Maas came up with the new paper, that day's, only a little messed up with Elaine's coffee stains. So naturally the old ones hit the floor and I dug into the BARTON BOMBING again.

And there was news! Yessir! Somebody'd sent the editors a letter claiming credit (that's what they called it) for our own little disaster; and the editors, who I've got to admit usually know a good story when they see it, hadn't just copied the words but had splashed a blow-up of the real thing over half of page five. Since the story (beginning page one, as they say) said it had come in the mail, my first idea was that it must've been written at least two weeks before the bomb. But no, "internal evidence" showed "clearly" that it had been done after the fact. I'd have liked to see the handwriting of somebody who'd set off a bomb in the middle of a crowd like that, and I'm sure the cops would've liked it too; but no such luck, the letter was typed. The funny thing, at least to me, was that it had been typed really well—a whole lot better than I could have done it myself. Naturally it was hard to be certain from a grainy newspaper photo, but I looked at every line as close as I could, and I couldn't find a single mistake.

Here's what it said:

To Whom It May Concern:

Our first attack at Barton was a <u>complete</u> success. Now bravely and cheerfully we will go on until the system that permits injustice is brought to it's knees. We are not by any means out of high explosives, and what we have <u>already</u> accomplished has brought in <u>several</u> new members. What we have done is no crime at all to those who have suffered as we have. We will no longer be slaves, instead we will be free.

Army of Independence

101

Aha, a clue!

Pretty often I get the feeling from talking to other people that when they read mysteries they pick the detectives they like best by peculiarities. Nero Wolfe's fat, three points; Sherlock Holmes shoots dope, that's seven. I don't. What I try to do is look at the way they find things out and solve their cases, and ask myself: *Does that make sense? Would it really work outside a book?*

And it seems to me that the best system I've ever read is just to look at the clues and think, now who would do that? If the murderer left his handkerchief behind, what kind of person would have that kind of handkerchief? Most men wouldn't have a colored one, for instance, but there's certain kinds that would. Some women's handkerchiefs are just about as useful as a man's, but a lot are only good for decorating your fingers when you're pretending to cry. A polka-dot bandanna with some nice, light perfume on it? It's not a gay cowboy, the killer is your own daring and talented author, Holly Hollander. Or somebody a lot like her.

So now I looked at the picture of that letter and tried to conjure up the person who wrote it. I would have liked to see the stationery, the watermark, and whether it was rag stock, but naturally I couldn't. From the picture, it was plain white and eight and a half by eleven. Not hotel stationery, or anybody's letterhead cut down, or drugstore paper with daisies and like that. School paper, like you buy to type your English themes, or office paper. The characters were so even it had to be an electric typewriter. The margins were wide, but the lines were single-spaced. I didn't know about other schools, but at Barton High they wanted you to double-space; it made it easier for the teachers to read and gave them room for spelling corrections and that kind of stuff.

Speaking of spelling, there was a goof in the letter: *it's* instead of *its*. A dumb, careless kind of mistake from some-body who could spell *independence* and *explosives* and *in-*

justice. An electric typewriter with a dictionary or maybe a word book lying alongside it. Whoever had written that letter had looked up the hard words, but he wasn't really a good speller or a grammatical writer. "We will no longer be slaves" was only weakened when he tacked "instead we will be free" onto the end.

"To whom it may concern" was kind of a boiler-plate phrase. Why didn't he just address it to the paper? He was planning to *send* it to the paper, after all; and he must have addressed an envelope and licked a stamp, and so forth. It made me think of a letter of recommendation: *To Whom It May Concern. Ms. Holly Hollander is a girl of excellent character who has never spent above two nights in jail. . . .*

Maybe whoever wrote it worked in an employment office, or maybe he was used to writing what Mrs. Maas called "characters" for himself. "Bravely and cheerfully" my foot!

Then it hit me—*for himself.* Right! All of a sudden I was perfectly sure there was only one of him, and all his talk about "we" and the "Army of Independence" was so much smoke. I still couldn't see his hands on the keyboard, much less his face—just the jumping typeball and the little book of forty thousand words spelled and divided. But he was all alone there, I knew that. No revolutionary committee had read his letter over. Nobody had suggested changes or simplifications or corrections. There was just him there in his little room, typing and underlining.

He underlined *a lot*—three words in just a few lines. It's supposed to be for emphasis, but I've noticed that people do it when they want to be ironic—I just *love* the way she treats me—or what's practically the same thing, when they want to convince somebody of something that isn't really true—I just *love* your new skirt! Okay, I'd already decided that the bit about *several* new members sounded fakey. (How would they know what to join, anyway?) So it seemed pretty likely that his other underlinings marked places where he wanted to put us on, too. The "attack" hadn't been a complete success then, something had gone wrong. And he didn't really plan to do *anything* else. (*Right here* I'm underlining for *emphasis!*)

That second part was good news for sure, but what had gone wrong? If he hadn't killed enough people, and hurt enough, it would stand to reason he'd want to try again. But I'd already decided he wasn't going to do that. So maybe what it was, was that he'd done *more* damage than he'd figured on; maybe he'd just wanted to scare everybody or something.

All that was okay, only when I got that far I was stuck. I looked and looked at that damn letter, and couldn't come up with another thing. After a while, though, it hit me that a lot of other people had to be looking at it just like I was—detectives and policemen all over, mystery fans like me, even some mystery writers; and that one of those people would be Blue. So I dug his card out of my billfold and gave him a call.

"Did you see it?" I said. "I mean the bomb letter. It's in today's paper."

"Yes, I've been studying it."

Then I gave him all my deductions just the way I've written them down here, only maybe not so well organized. (You may have noticed that I'm usually better organized when I write than when I talk; when I talk I try to say it all at once.)

"I agree," Blue said when I was finished.

"With all of it?"

"Yes. That is to say, I agree that all you've guessed is possible, though none of it is provable. We don't really know, for example, that whoever wrote the letter was an expert typist. It's conceivable that the writer carefully struck one key at a time, beginning again and again until at last a perfect copy was achieved. But it's not likely. The most probable answer is the one you've given, and we should cling to it until there's reason to doubt it.

"The business about 'To Whom It May Concern' seems

quite a bit more chancy, although what you say is as convincing as any other possibility and more helpful than most; you must remember, however, that we don't know the letter was mailed by the person who composed it. That's conjecture, too, though again it's sound conjecture. In addition, we don't know that the copy mailed to the newspaper was the only copy sent out. Suppose that carbons were made, to be mailed to the police? Or suppose that the copy the newspaper received is a photostat? They don't say that it is, and the article seems to imply that it is the original; but the article may be deceptive."

Call me Practical Pig. "Isn't there some way we can find out?"

"I have a friend at the paper—"

"I figured you would."

"Who's promised to call me back to clear up several points, including that one. When he does, I'd like to speak with you. I've turned up certain facts that I think may interest you. Is your father home yet?"

" 'Fraid not. Maybe tomorrow." I was hoping he would be, but the truth was I didn't have the least idea. "Just the same, I'd like to see you."

"You will," he said, and hung up. I had put down the phone before it hit me that I'd told him all the stuff I'd figured out but he hadn't told me any of his—just showed me how some things I'd said could be wrong, even if I was sure they weren't. He hadn't said when he might be along, either. Naturally he didn't know, because he was waiting for his newspaper friend to call, but that didn't make me any less mad. I sat up in bed turning the pages of that damned old paper till I'd convinced myself he wouldn't come at all, and then I nearly cried.

Mrs. Maas brought up a tray with cocoa (I'm a cocoa addict) and a chop, and spinach and lyonnaise potatoes, and my absolute top favorite of all desserts, which is strawberry shortcake with a buttered beaten biscuit for the shortcake.

Then I *did* cry, and Mrs. Maas kissed my forehead like Glinda the Good and said, "There, there"; but she thought it was just my leg and so on. But all of a sudden I knew it was because I had remembered one time when Larry had picked up Megan and Les and me in his van and taken us to a greasy spoon on Highway 14. They'd had Cokes or Mr. Pibb or something, but Larry and I'd had cocoa, which he'd called "hot chocolate."

Now Larry was dead, truly dead, rotting in a funeral parlor in a coffin with the top nailed down, and I would never be able to drink cocoa again without thinking of him a little bit, and I had never really cried for him before.

It felt good; it felt like there had been this round, hard, bitter thing down below my heart all this time, and the tears that really soaked into my sheet went down there somehow and melted it.

Pretty soon I heard a beater (that's an old junker that rattles and rumbles) out front, and I knew that it would be Aladdin Blue. By the time he'd made it up the stairs I was scarfing my chop just as nice as you please.

He said, "How's the invalid?" and I said, "What did you find out from your pal on the paper?"

"It was the typed original they got, not a xerographic copy or a carbon—that was the point you were interested in."

"Do you think it was really terrorists? I guess that's a dumb question, since every murderer's a terrorist, more or less. Every murder scares us, anyway."

"No," Blue answered. "No, I don't think this murderer is a terrorist, much less one of a secret band of terrorists—though I might be wrong. And, no, not every murderer is a terrorist. Most are not. A terrorist has as his chief aim the excitation of fear, usually for political or quasi-political reasons. If a bank robber shoots one teller to intimidate the rest, you could call him a terrorist, I suppose. But it's only in one case out of a hundred that a bank robber does that;

the other ninety-nine who shoot tellers do it because they themselves are frightened, with or without reason. They are terrorized, and not terrorists, even though their fears are the result of their own acts. Most murderers don't even want to excite our fears—they would be far happier if they could get their victims out of the way without our noticing, which is why they often go to considerable lengths to conceal them, or to make us believe they died by accident or disease."

"Whoever killed Larry Lief certainly didn't do that."

There was only one chair in my bedroom besides the vanity stool, a chintzy thing I never found very comfortable. Blue was in it now, his hands on the handle of his stick.

"On the contrary," he said slowly, "in some sense that may have been exactly what Larry's killer did. Terrorism is a sort of disease in our society, and we're supposed to believe poor Larry died of it."

"Is it the one who made those phone calls?"

Blue shook his head. "Larry may have been killed because of something that took place in Vietnam, or he may have been killed just because he happened to be in the wrong spot at the right time. But both those things can't be true together. No, I don't believe that the hand that directed that shell at him was the one that dialed those calls. I never have."

"Shell?" I must have looked as wiped out as I felt.

"I should have told you sooner. The shrapnel they dug out of the casualties made it plain enough when they got a bit of it together—that's what Sandoz was talking about when he said that he had evidence that showed there was no bomb in Pandora's Box. Now his men have found the baseplate. Larry was killed—and you were injured—by the explosion of an artillery shell."

107

14
How Blue Got That Way

"YOU'RE crazy!" I said. "You are stark, staring nuts!"

"No, not at all." Blue was smiling his littlest smile, one that's mostly in his eyes. "You'll find the story in tomorrow's *Tribune*—my information comes from my friend there, not from the police; an enterprising reporter caught a leak at the ballistics lab, presumably."

"Somebody shot at them—shot at us—with a cannon? That's crazy!" As you may have noticed, I pride myself on originality. The truth was that I was still trying to take it in. Every time I got it past my ears, my head tossed it out.

"So it seems."

"Then that would tie right in with Vietnam! Look, suppose Larry was in the artillery there, see? And he added a bunch of numbers wrong, so they aimed too low and killed somebody's best friend. Now the other friend gets him back."

Blue shook his head. "I don't think so. I believe that I mentioned that they found the baseplate. Do you know what that is?"

"What they put the gun on to fire it, I suppose."

"You're thinking of the baseplate of a mortar, a different thing with the same name. The baseplate of an artillery shell is a thick metal section that separates the explosive inside the shell from the gunpowder that will propel it. When the shell explodes, most of its casing shatters into the ragged and deadly scraps we call shrapnel—or when they come from an antiaircraft gun, flak. The base plate is too strong to fragment like that, however; it has to be, in order to prevent the firing of the gun from setting off the charge in the shell. If the baseplate can be found, an ordnance expert can usually determine exactly what type of shell it came from. This one was made for an artillery piece that to the best of my knowledge wasn't used in Vietnam at all: a World War Two German eighty-eight."

"That still doesn't prove it had nothing to do with Vietnam," I argued. "If there were some guys who wanted to kill Larry, they couldn've stolen the gun from a museum or something. Anyway, they sure couldn't have brought their own gun back with them, and maybe they were willing to take anything they could get. Hell, they'd have to be."

"If it's any comfort to you, Lieutenant Sandoz appears to agree with you. He has a crew of men looking at possible sites for such a gun—it would have to have been within a mile or two of the school—and another team looking for the gun itself, in abandoned quarries and so forth."

"And you're not doing that."

"Why should I?" Blue asked. "They have an army: deputies, state troopers, God knows what. If there's a deserted spot that can be reached by road within range of that high school, they'll find it. If the gun's within a hundred miles of here and hasn't already been melted down for scrap, they'll find that."

"Only you don't think they will."

Blue shrugged. "At this point I don't know what to think. Please notice that I never said I believed anything so fantastic occurred; I merely said that the police seem to. Yet they have evidence. Conceivably, that shell might have been thrown from some kind of catapult or dropped from a plane, but those ideas are as bad as the gun. Worse."

"Wait a minute," I said, and then I told him about the old lady's house where we'd gone in for lemonade. "Naturally she'd notice if somebody shot a cannon in her front yard," I finished, "but she must leave home sometimes, and come to think of it, she said she might come to the Fair this year. If she did, she'd have been gone, and I'm certain she was living there alone."

Blue waved a hand and stood up. I think that may have been the first time I ever saw him pace, which is something he only does when he's really upset. He goes up and down dragging his bad leg behind him and hitting the floor with his stick like he wants to kill it. I hate it. I hated it then, the first time. He makes me think of a cougar in a nature film I saw once; this cougar had pulled loose the trap that had caught it and it was trying to get away, to go somewhere far off in the woods where horrible things didn't happen, and it was dragging that damned trap with it all the time. When I close my eyes, the thump of Blue's stick makes me think maybe there really is a trap on his crippled leg, one that neither of us can see.

"I'll grant that," Blue said, still talking about the old lady's being gone. "Certainly if she wasn't out, various tricks could have been used to get her out of the house—burglars have developed a whole bagful of them, from a telephone call warning the victim of some imaginary natural disaster to theater tickets supposedly sent by a business contact. Even if she wasn't away, she could have been drugged, or silenced by threats. It's the gun itself I can't accept. If it had been a rocket launcher or a recoilless rifle, it might be possible; but a weapon that size would have to be transported in a large truck, or towed behind one. Did you notice how you spoke of 'guys,' even though only a few minutes ago you told me you felt sure the killer had worked alone? That was because you realized instinctively that several people would be required to arrange something like this. A gun crew. The thing's preposterous."

Just then the phone by my bed rang. When I hung up, Blue was back in my chintz chair, smiling. "My father's on his way home," I told him.

"I'm delighted to hear it."

"That was Bill. He took Elaine someplace and dropped her off. My father just called from O'Hare. He's going to get a bite to eat there while Bill drives over to pick him up."

"That shouldn't take long," Blue said. "An hour and a half at the outside, if they don't get stuck in traffic."

"You've been wanting to meet him, haven't you?" My hands were already smoothing out the sheet, even though I knew it was silly.

"I'd like to get a retainer from him if I can."

"It would be useful, wouldn't it? Like the stuff you told Sandoz so he'd let you stay in my room at the hospital."

Blue shook his head. "I need the money. The money would be useful, if you want to put it that way. I've been looking at your bookcases—Fleming, Chandler, MacDonald. You're fond of mysteries."

"I've got Poe and Van Dine and Sir Arthur Conan Doyle here on the other side," I told him. "Historical grounding. And I have a soft spot for Ellery Queen, even if he'd be older than my father if he were real."

Blue sniffed. "You ought to find a detective your own age. But I was going to quote Chandler to you, and I still will. He wrote, 'Down these mean streets a man must go who is not himself mean, who is neither tarnished nor afraid.' "

I interrupted to say, "You've read him too—harder than I did."

"I've had more time. Chandler was concerned with honor and not with money—that word *tarnished* is an indirect reference to knightly armor. This though Marlowe was born in the Depression, when even such a man, honorable, intelligent, brave, and tough, might have a difficult time earning a living; and though Raymond Chandler was concerned with honor, Philip Marlowe was concerned about money. He had to be. If you've read those books with any insight, you know that he's a creature of the thirties, and the earliest forties, before the Second World War broke the back of the crash of twenty-nine forever. The real Philip Marlowe died in nineteen forty-one, not on a battlefield but in a thousand defense plants."

"You're not a private eye." I believe in getting right to the point. After all, if I didn't my supply of enemies might run out.

"I'm not a private detective because I couldn't possibly get a license. I can call myself a criminologist and offer my services as a consultant because I have a degree in criminology. I earned that degree in prison."

"You did time?"

Blue nodded emphatically. I think he wanted to make sure I couldn't say later that I hadn't known. "Five years and some odd months. I should have told you sooner: you are consorting with a felon."

"You used to be a lawyer."

He looked surprised. "That's correct. How did you know?"

"Just a hunch. When we went out to Garden Meadow, you were going to see somebody who'd been a judge. Later Sandoz said you looked like a lawyer, and just then you sounded like one."

"I was disbarred, of course." Blue leaned back in the chintz chair and closed his eyes, his stick lying across his lap. "The career I planned . . ."

For about as long as it takes to open a package of gum,

112

everything got perfectly quiet. Downstairs someplace I could hear Mrs. Maas running the sweeper.

"I never wanted to go into politics," Blue said at last. "Or to go on the bench. But I was going to be a bigger trial lawyer than F. Lee Bailey or Clarence Darrow. Now here I am."

"*Perry Mason!*"

Blue opened his eyes and looked at me. "Just what do you mean by that?"

"I mean you're as big a sucker for mysteries as I am. You wanted to be Perry Mason."

"I suppose so."

"Well, what happened? Tell me about it."

"It isn't very complicated. A certain man—a professional criminal—wanted me to defend him. I took the case, even though I felt sure he was guilty of worse crimes if he was innocent of the one he had been charged with. I needed the money, and after all everyone is entitled to counsel, guilty or innocent.

"At the trial I did the best I could for him, but it became increasingly clear that he would be convicted. He asked me to bribe the judge—not to find him not guilty, which would've been impossible anyway since it was a jury trial, but to give him a light sentence."

"Why didn't he do it himself?"

"He was out on bail, but he was being watched by the police—more and more closely as it became apparent that the verdict would go against him. The few associates he had whom he could have trusted with something of that sort were being watched as well, some because they were his associates and some for other reasons. He insisted that I do it. He was a very forceful man, strong physically and strong of will. Someone once said that all strong men are good-natured—or that if they are not, the people around them are, which comes to the same thing."

"So you did it?"

Blue shook his head, a very slight shake this time; I don't think the end of that sharp nose moved half an inch. "Not then. I told him he would have to find someone else if he wanted to go through with it, and that if he did I didn't want to know about it. And then that if he continued to try to force me into it, I would have to resign the case."

"I'm surprised he didn't just go out and hire himself a crooked lawyer."

"There are never enough of those to meet the demand," Blue said. "Besides, most of them aren't as crooked as people think. They are small crooks, who might hint to a juror's wife that her husband would soon have a better job if things went well. This was serious. It involved a judge who needed money, and a great deal of cash in unmarked bills.

"Then too, Holly, you have to understand that most crooked lawyers aren't very good lawyers. That's why they're crooked, basically—they can't earn much of a living otherwise. I was a good lawyer, or at least I thought I was, and my client thought so too; he wanted me for *his* crooked lawyer. That's one way in which lawyers are made crooked, you see. Once I had tendered that bribe, he would have me in his pocket for the rest of my life. I would have to do whatever I could to pull him out of any legal difficulty he got into, because if he thought I had not done enough and he went to prison, he would tell; then the judge and I would both have been finished."

"But you said no."

"Yes, I told him no. Two or three nights later—I forget just how long it was—I received a telephone call. It was a woman's voice. The woman said she had information relating to another case of mine. She would not come to my apartment, but she offered to meet me in an all-night drugstore not far from where I lived. As I was walking toward the drugstore, a man in a raincoat came toward me. When we were close, he opened his raincoat." Blue paused, and the little smile came back. "I remember that I wondered for an instant whether he was a flasher—whether he intended to expose himself. What he actually had beneath his raincoat wasn't an erection but a sawed-off shotgun. He fired at my legs, and the next thing I knew I was lying facedown on the sidewalk, bleeding."

"I dig it," I said.

"Yes, you've been there yourself, haven't you? The judge granted a continuance, of course, and my client came to visit me in the hospital. He was very friendly. He told me that he had not wanted to do what he had, but that if I refused to do as I was told he would kill me. And it suddenly came to me that the whole system of the law, which I had studied and supported, had done nothing and would do nothing to protect me from this man. As soon as I was able to hobble about, I went to see the judge."

"And?"

"He wouldn't take it. It was that simple. By that time he had found the racehorse thing—though I didn't know that at the time—which was far safer and got him all the money he required. He told me to come back with the cash, and when I did there were two FBI agents in the next room videotaping everything. He was a federal judge; I should have told you that. My client went to prison, and so did I. So did the judge himself, about two years later."

"That was the judge you went to see at Garden Meadow, then. You said he'd been in jail."

Blue nodded. "He feels he owes me something, because he turned me in when he was acting dishonestly himself. I don't agree, but I value his friendship.

"At any rate, all that is another story; I set out to tell you about my studies. It's possible to do college work in most of our prisons, and I did. I knew I would need a new profession when I was released, and the only things I could really learn where I was were penology and criminology. Anything else would have been a matter of acquiring a theoretical background without practical experience. By devoting my studies to criminology, I turned my prison time to my own benefit, if you like."

I asked him how it had felt, majoring in criminology while he was surrounded by criminals, and we talked about that till my father came.

15

How My Father Got Smart

IT was really hell when my father came home, because I wanted to jump up and run out and kiss him, and I couldn't. I heard the Caddy's tires crunch the gravel, then the front door rattle, then the deep growl of his voice when he said hello to Mrs. Maas, and finally the scrape of his shoes on the stairs, and all that time I had to sit there like a dummy.

Then the door opened, and there he was. I yelled, "Daddy!" and held out my arms and he came over and gave me a squeeze, and just for a second there I caught the spicy smell of his aftershave. He looked like he always had, only maybe a little more tired and worried.

Aladdin Blue was starting to stand up to shake hands, so my father said, "No, no. Keep your seat." But Blue got up just the same and they shook.

"Mr. Blue is a criminologist," I said.

"I know. Mr. Blue called me at the Plaza, I believe." My father looked at Blue. When he doesn't want you to, you can't ever tell whether he likes what he sees. "You aren't associated with the police?"

"No," Blue said. "As I told you then, I'm associated with the crime. I was at the Fair, chatting with your daughter, when the explosion occurred."

"I know," my father said again. "Your leg . . ."

"That's an old injury."

I said, "He was shot by gangsters," which I *still* think was a diplomatic thing to say under the circumstances, although Blue gave me a look that would have set fire to a pile of bricks.

"You weren't injured by the blast, Mr. Blue?"

"I was lucky. Your daughter was sitting by a window, and wasn't equally lucky. I was also stupid. I ran—as near as I can come to running—out of the building without realizing she had been hurt. A shard of glass wounded her; she can tell you about it."

"I'm sure she will, but I'm keeping you standing." My father turned to me. "Holly, I see some crutches in the corner. Can you walk?"

"A little," I said.

"How did you get upstairs?"

"Bill carried me."

"If Bill could carry you up, I can carry you down. I want to continue this in my study, where Mr. Blue and I can sit down, and I can offer him a good cigar and a drink. I'd like a drink myself."

The way it turned out, I hobbled on my crutches—aluminum jobs Elaine had rented at the hospital—as far as the top of the stairs, and my father picked me up there and carried me down and through the foyer, with Blue limping on ahead of us to open the study door.

I mentioned the study when I told about going in there to have a look at the letter from Garden Meadow, but I didn't tell too much about it. It wasn't a big room as rooms in our place went, although I'm sure that in lots of nice homes it would be the biggest room in the house. About fifteen by twenty, maybe. The door was at one end, and there was a bow window looking out onto some japonica and grass and other stuff (I don't know what you're supposed to call it) at the other. On the right wall was a big fieldstone fireplace with white birch logs stacked beside it. Sometimes my father had a fire there in the winter. The walls were paneled with some kind of nearly black wood— it was American walnut, I think—that I liked. There was no light in the ceiling, so it seemed kind of dark and cozy in there even with the desk light and both floor lamps on. Besides the desk, there were bookcases, a big library table, a coffee table, a wet bar, a little brown leather sofa (which was where my father set me down) and brown leather easy chairs.

"Drink?" my father asked Blue.

Blue nodded and said, "Whatever you're having," which meant he got Chivas and soda. I got a gin rickey minus the gin, which was what I always got when my father mixed drinks. I didn't get offered a cigar (I would have taken it) and Blue waved his away. I wondered if he knew it was a Ruiz y Blanco, made by people who skipped out of Cuba when Castro took over.

"You don't object to my smoking, I hope?"

Blue shook his head, and my father lit up. I thought about Lieutenant Sandoz then, because both of them turned their cigars to get the fire even.

"When I spoke to you by telephone, I told you everything I knew about the case at the time," Blue said, "but there've been several interesting developments since."

"The bombing, you mean."

Blue nodded.

"I'm not concerned with the bombing, Mr. Blue. I tried to make that clear earlier."

Blue glanced at me. "Your daughter was one of the victims, Mr. Hollander." It was the first time he'd called my father anything. I got the feeling he'd come to some kind of decision when he said that.

119

"I know it, and unless you have children of your own you'll never understand how much I regret that. But Holly was hurt as anyone else might have been hurt; in fact, as a good many others actually were. If these radicals had put a bomb on an airplane instead, and I had been killed with two hundred other passengers, I wouldn't expect my family or my friends to discover just which lunatic had built the bomb or who had checked the fatal suitcase on board. That's badly put, but perhaps you see what I mean."

Blue nodded again. "I believe I do."

"The crime I'm concerned about, the crime that has brought me back at an exceedingly inconvenient time, is the murder of my brother Bert."

"I ought to have expressed my sympathy sooner," Blue said. "In any event, I extend it now. I can't resist adding, however, that your brother's murder is one of the developments to which I referred."

My father's eyebrows went up. I bet he looks that way when somebody asks for a raise. "You believe the two are connected, Mr. Blue?"

"They appear to be, yes."

I must have made some sort of a noise, sucked air, maybe, because they both looked at me and I felt dumb. Then my father said, "I admit that I probably don't know as much about this as you do. Not only because I lack your training, but because you have been on the spot and I haven't. In my business, I've found it's the man on the spot whose opinions can be relied upon. But from what I do know, those events seem completely unrelated. My daughter was injured by some fanatic's bomb, while Bert was—"

He broke off and wiped his forehead. "Good Lord! I don't even know how he died. Joan called from the office and told me he'd been murdered in some parking lot. What happened? Was he shot? Stabbed?"

I put in, "On TV they said he'd been shot with a thirty-eight."

HOW MY FATHER GOT SMART

My father looked relieved, as if knowing how his brother had died made it easier somehow. Maybe it did.

Blue added, "He was shot only once, in the chest, and died almost instantly. He can hardly have known what was happening. Someone—presumably his murderer—dragged his body about fifteen feet to conceal it in shrubbery."

"A mugger?"

"No. The police thought so at first, because there was no watch and no wallet. I was able to demonstrate to them that it was much more probable that those things were never present to begin with. Your brother—as we both know—had escaped from a private mental hospital."

My father gave me a Look, and I signaled back *no* good and hard.

Blue said, "I sometimes visit a friend at the same hospital, Mr. Hollander. I met your brother several times, and recognized his name at once when I heard it over the police shortwave. The point I wanted to make is that most patients there don't bother to wear watches—I've verified this with my friend—and have no reason to carry wallets. They are not permitted currency, and whatever identification they may have is locked away."

"A mugger couldn't have known that."

Blue nodded. "Of course not. But when a mugger kills his victim it is usually by accident—he strikes him on the head, and in the excitement of the moment strikes too hard. Or the victim resists and is stabbed in the melee. One seldom hears of a mugger who shoots his victims in cold blood so he can loot the corpse afterward, and it would seem to be a poorly thought-out technique. Pistols are noisy."

My father drew on his cigar; he was looking at the ceiling. "Bert might have rushed him just the same. Bert was like that. Suppose this mugger drew his gun—"

"Technically," Blue interrupted, "that word *gun* indicates an artillery piece. Let's call it a pistol."

If my father knew that an artillery shell had exploded at

the Fair, he sure didn't let on. For a minute there I thought
he was going to get angry because Blue was quibbling; then
he smiled. "That's right. How did it go? 'This is my rifle,
and this is my gun. This's for shooting, this other's for fun.' "

The smile turned to a grin when he looked at me. "I won't
explain that, Holly. G.I. poetry."

"You're correct, of course," Blue went on. "It's possible
a mugger approached your brother in that parking lot,
pointed a pistol at him and demanded his money, and your
brother tried to take his weapon from him. I don't believe
it, but it is barely possible."

"Why don't you believe it, Mr. Blue?"

"There are at least three reasons. The first is that your
brother appears to have been shot while standing fully erect.
If he had died while rushing at his assailant, the bullet would
have entered his chest an an angle; a man bends forward
when he runs or leaps at his enemy."

"You've seen his body?"

Blue nodded.

"Suppose he had grasped the other man's arm. The two
of them might have been wrestling for the pistol."

"In that case, there would have been severe powder burns
around the wound. There were powder burns, but they were
light, indicating that the muzzle of the weapon was at least
a foot away from him when it was fired."

My father got quiet for a minute or two, then he said,
"All right, you said you had three reasons. What's the second?"

Blue shook his head. "You won't like it."

"I want to hear it."

"Aside from a few coins, only one object was found in
your brother's pockets. It was a bloodstained paper rose."

"I'm afraid I don't understand. What's the significance of
that?"

"When I was talking with your daughter just before the

bomb went off, she was wearing a red flower in her hair. When I saw her after the explosion, her hair was disheveled and the flower was gone. Your brother had come to that room, looking for her, once. He must have come again—perhaps hours, but perhaps only minutes, after the explosion. He found that flower, recognized it, and picked it up. He learned where she had been taken."

"In other words, he was on his way to see her when he was killed. I'd assumed that."

"I do not assume it," Blue said, "but it seems clear to me that your daughter's injury and your brother's death are linked, and that eliminates simple robbery as a motive."

"And your third reason?"

"Because you don't believe it yourself, Mr. Hollander. Your daughter was injured, as I informed you by telephone. She was still alive, and thus in need of whatever comfort you might have provided her. You were involved in an important business matter and did not come. Then your brother was killed. He is beyond all human aid, yet you came at once."

"I had intended to come anyway," my father said. "By last night matters in New York appeared a good deal less urgent than I had thought earlier."

"One of the first things you said when we entered this room was, 'The crime I am concerned about, the crime that has brought me back at an exceedingly inconvenient time, is the murder of my brother Bert.'"

"You have a good memory."

Blue nodded. "Yes, I do. You don't deny you said that?"

"I'm sure I did, or something like it. You're right, of course; I was testing the water. You've offered your services as a criminologist, Mr. Blue. Very well, I accept—I want you to investigate the death of my brother."

Blue shut up for a minute; then he said, "We criminologists don't make investigations, Mr. Hollander; if we did, we would be private investigators. We study crime, and criminals. On one condition, I will undertake such a study of the death of Herbert Hollander the Third."

"The law intrudes on everything today, doesn't it. What's your condition?"

"That I be retained as a consultant by the Hollander Safe and Lock Company Incorporated, and not by you as an individual. You understand, I'm sure, that the association with your company may be professionally advantageous to me."

"I was about to suggest it myself. This way we can write it off as a business expense. How much?" My father was getting a pad of Hollander Safe & Lock checks out of his desk.

"Five thousand," Blue said. "That will get us started."

My father paused. He always did, whether it was sixty-five bucks for a shirt or sixty-five thousand for a new bracelet for Elaine. "All right," he said. "It will be worth it if you can clear this thing up." And there was no way to tell whether he would have called it off at six or gone into five figures.

As he passed the check over, there was a familiar tap on the door. I sang out, "What is it, Mrs. Maas?" and she said, "Tell Mr. Hollander there are some policemen here looking for Mrs. Hollander."

16

How Lieutenant Sandoz
Named the Killer

OKAY, it's time to come clean—I'm psychic. You remember when I watched my father firing up his cigar, and it reminded me of Lieutenant Sandoz of the Pool County Cops? Well, *at that very moment* the real Sandoz must have been on his way to our house. Makes you think, doesn't it? Astral bodies, life after death, and all that stuff. There are people selling articles to the supermarket tabloids on the strength of a lot less.

And just in case you're still not convinced, when Sandoz introduced himself and sat down in my father's study— taking the last chair, I might add, so that the benighted shlepper with him had to stand—he turned down my father's offer of a good cigar and lit one of his own, a stogie made in New Jersey by refugees from Appalachia, by the smell of it.

"My housekeeper says you're looking for my wife," my father said. "She's out shopping, I think."

Sandoz nodded. "We'd like to speak with Mrs. Hollander, yes."

"I certainly hope you're not such a fool as to think that Mrs. Hollander has . . ." My father let it hang there.

"Killed somebody?" Sandoz didn't smile—not even the tiny turning of his mouth that he probably called a smile. He wasn't being funny and he wasn't being cute, or at least he didn't want us to think he was.

"I wasn't going to go nearly that far. Been involved in any serious illegality."

"No," Sandoz said. Then, "Maybe you might want to get your daughter and your man Blue out of here."

"You wish to speak to me in confidence?"

Sandoz shook his head. "Maybe you want to speak to me in confidence."

"If this concerns the murder of my brother, I'd like his niece, and Mr. Blue, to hear whatever is said."

"No, this concerns the death of Lawrence L. Lief of Barton. There are two others involved, too. Mr. Drexel K. Munroe and Mrs. Edith A. Simmons—"

(So one of us wounded had finally died.)

"—but specifically and particularly Mr. Lawrence L. Lief."

"In that case, it doesn't concern me or my family, as I was just explaining to Mr. Blue. I don't want to discuss it, except over a dinner table."

There was a long pause. Then Sandoz said, "Mr. Hollander, I would like your permission to search this house."

Blue put in, "Have you got a warrant?"

Lieutenant Sandoz swung his wooden puss toward him. "If I had a warrant, I wouldn't have to ask permission; you know that. I'm asking Mr. Hollander to permit a search of these premises, to show that he's dealing in good faith with the police."

My father said, "I'm not anxious to show any kind of faith to the police—good or bad. At this point, I owe nothing to the police, and I suggest to you that if the police were to spend half the energy they put into molesting reputable people into searching for the radicals who killed Larry Lief and the thug who murdered my brother, nothing more would be required."

Sandoz lifted his shoulders. "You refuse."

"Absolutely."

"All right. We'll have to go to a judge for a warrant now, and it's better if we can tell the judge we asked and permission was denied. I'd like to use your phone, but if you want to be a bastard about it, Jake will go out to the car and radio someone, and they'll phone. You want to be a bastard?"

"There's a telephone in the hall," my father said. "You can use that."

"There's one here, too. It's closer."

If I'd had my brain going, I would have reached over and grabbed the phone cord and pulled the phone off the desk so he'd have had to get up and bend over to get it. It wouldn't have accomplished anything, but it would have made me feel better. Only I didn't. I got caught flat-footed (if you can get caught flat-footed when your feet aren't in working order) and Sandoz had the phone before I thought of it. He pushed buttons for a number that must have rung three or four times. Then he said, "He's here. . . . Yeah, back from New York. Tell them. . . . He won't do it. . . . That's right, tell Dugan we asked, and he says no dice. . . ." He listened for a while longer, then grunted and hung up. "We'll have a man out here with a warrant in about an hour."

My father said, "I doubt that. But whether it's true or not, in the meantime you can leave my house. I believe I'm within my rights in ordering the police off private property."

Sandoz nodded. "If we don't have a warrant, that's right. But, Mr. Hollander, I have a good deal to say that you might find interesting."

"I don't—"

127

"And if we leave, you're coming with us. Jake and I are going to talk to you in one place or another, if you understand what I mean."

"You would arrest me?"

"Not unless we had to. First we'd ask you come down, as any citizen might do, to give evidence to the police. If you decided to be a bastard . . ." Sandoz shrugged again.

My father said, "If I give evidence at this point, it will be with my attorney present."

"I figured that. You've heard of the Miranda decision, Mr. Hollander?"

"I've heard the term, yes—I think on some television show. I know nothing about the details."

"I wouldn't expect you to. It's been my experience—I know Mr. Blue there is an expert and maybe he'll want to argue with me—but it's been my experience as a plain country cop that one big difference between a pro and an amateur is that the pro does his homework. Most pros aren't smart— a smart man doesn't take up crime as a career unless there's special circumstances. Lots of times the amateurs are. Not long ago, just to give you an example, we got a kid who'd raped and strangled three college girls, and he turned out to be an honor student at Pool County College. We got him because before he killed the third one he took her to some disco joint. You ask yourself, why would a smart kid like him do a dumb thing like that?"

Sandoz blew a thick stream of smoke out of each nostril and looked around at us. "I think it was because he just couldn't imagine that we'd ever get onto him enough to go around with his picture and her picture. He thought that. we'd never get close to him. A pro would have said to himself, what if they get onto me? A pro knows about Miranda and all the rest of it—better, sometimes, than we do.

"What Miranda does is make us read you a whole bunch of rights when we arrest you. I don't mean you specifically, Mr. Hollander—whoever we might have to arrest. We've

128

got to tell them they don't have to answer, and they've got the right to a lawyer, and so forth. Now I want to be as open with you as I can, so I'm telling you all these things even though you're not under arrest yet. If you want to hear it, I'll also tell you why I think I may have to place you under arrest."

My father said, "I want to hear it." He looked grim.

"That's fine. You see, I want to show you we're not being unreasonable. We're not out to get you, we're out to get the perpetrator. If that happens to be you—and personally I think it does—then that's your fault and not ours. So far this is all hypothetical."

"If you have something to say, say it."

"Sure, and I'll make it as short as I can. To begin with, everything depends on two assumptions I've made. If either of them's wrong, everything falls through. Maybe one *is* wrong. Maybe they both are. The first one is that the two crimes are connected, which is to say that the explosion at the school in Barton is tied to the shooting of Herbert Hollander the Third."

"I don't agree with that."

"Well, I think it's true just the same, and maybe if I tell you why, you'll agree with me. In police work, Mr. Hollander, we're always looking for similarities. A man that breaks into groceries, for instance, usually does it again and again. If you've got two burglaries, and one's at the A and P and the other's at a Jewel, you usually find that the same guy did them both. You see what I mean. So I've been looking at these killings and trying to match things up. Let's look at the second one first, because it's so much simpler. Herbert Hollander the Third was killed, and there doesn't seem to be any doubt that he was the guy the killer meant to get. The shooting took place at night, sure, but that parking lot was lit up pretty good—we checked it out. The murderer was close, too, when he fired, and he was looking at your brother Herbert head on. When Cain killed Abel with the rock, he probably didn't see him much better."

Sandoz waited to give my father a chance to say something. When he didn't, he went on. "One thing I've thought about was whether maybe—just maybe—Herbert Hollander was mistaken for his brother, George Henry Hollander."

"If I killed him myself, that's hardly possible, is it?"

Sandoz nodded, being fair. "That's what I thought, too. But I'd already turned it down for a couple of other reasons. Nobody who knew you could have mistaken your brother for you in that lot. He was an older man, and a taller man, and a slimmer man. Your hair's gray; his was white, and he wasn't wearing a hat. If anybody made that mistake, it would have to be somebody who didn't know you—a hit man working from a verbal description or maybe a picture. Well, there are a dozen real pros operating out of Chicago who'll give you a nice slick job for the price of a new car, and lights in a parking lot wouldn't even slow those boys down—I've known them to blow away their man in the middle of one of those expense-account restaurants, with a roomful of customers and waiters watching. What I couldn't figure out is why one would be hanging around the parking lot waiting to shoot your brother by mistake. When that guy got hit that I told you about, the guy in the restaurant, it was because somebody'd fingered him. Who fingered you? Nobody, if you were really in New York like you said you were."

"I was."

"I hope so, Mr. Hollander. You have somebody with you? We think your brother was shot between one-thirty and two-thirty in the morning. That estimate's from the coroner's office, based on their examination of the corpse. That would be two-thirty to three-thirty in New York."

"No, I had nobody with me. I was asleep in my room in the hotel."

"Uh huh. I kind of thought you might say that. You know, Mr. Hollander, it's a wonderful age we live in. These days it only takes a couple of hours to fly from New York to Chicago, and a couple more to fly back. Suppose a man said good night to his business associates at eleven P.M. New York time and went up to his room. Why, at eleven-thirty he could sneak out of the hotel, and by twelve-thirty he could be at some airport easy—not much traffic at that time of night. By two-thirty—this is still New York time—he'd be in Chicago. If he had his business finished by three-thirty, New York time, he'd be back at his hotel before seven. There's not many people up and around in the average hotel at six or six-thirty. He'd probably be able to catch a few hours' sleep, even, on the planes, and in his hotel room before he had to show his face somewhere. He'd look a little tired of course—circles under the eyes and so on—but people would probably expect that, if he'd been working hard and they knew his little daughter, his only child, had just been hurt.

"Then too, there's the business about the hospital parking lot. That looks bad, like I said, for a hit man. But it looks just fine for a relative. Herbert Hollander had jumped the wall at the funny farm, but he wasn't so crazy us cops didn't have a hard time laying hands on him. He could walk down a street, and he could talk to people, and nobody'd know he was supposed to be in an institution. Suppose he called his brother in New York. Asking for help, maybe."

My father shook his head. "He didn't."

"I'm just supposing. Like I told you, so far this is all hypothetical.

"Well, what would be more natural than for the brother to say, 'I'm just now leaving for Chicago to see about Holly. Meet me in the parking lot—not in the lobby, where they might spot you and send you back—and I'll give you the money for a ticket to Tahiti.' Or whatever it was his brother had said he wanted." Sandoz spread his big, hard-looking brown hands. "You see what I mean? It falls into place pretty good.

"So it was Herbert Hollander that got killed, and it was him that was meant to be killed. All right, how about the other killing, the cannon shell that exploded at Barton High?"

"Cannon shell?" My father's face was so tight it seemed like somebody was standing behind him pulling at the skin.

Sandoz drew on his cigar. "Didn't you think we knew about that? Yes, sir, an old shell from a German Army gun. We know who was killed when it went off, but I asked myself there, too, if they were meant to be killed. Mrs. Simmons was farther away than several people that haven't died, so I think we can forget about her. We've dug around a bit on Mr. Munroe without coming up with a better-than-average reason somebody'd want him dead."

I said, "What about the guys from Vietnam who were out to get Larry, you dumb S.O.B.?"

Sandoz looked at me and smiled a little. "That's a good question, Miss Hollander, and to tell the truth I don't even much mind the way you asked it. These days it's kind of nice to find out there are still kids around who get upset when somebody calls their old man a murderer. I can't tell you anything about those guys from Vietnam, except that they're so hard to locate that I'm beginning to wonder if they're real at all."

17

How Sandoz Pulled a Gun

"HEY, wait a minute," I said. "I saw them. I told you about that when you came to see me in the hospital."

Sandoz shook his head. "You saw a car pull away from the curb, Miss Hollander, after you'd heard a story that scared you a little bit. Tell ten girls your age a ghost story and stick them in an old house, and at least three will see a ghost. All of them will hear something that might have been one."

"But—"

"We've looked high and low for the place where these people might have had their cannon, and there isn't any. What's more conclusive, to me at least, is that we've talked over the phone with about twenty men who knew Lief in Vietnam. Some of them we got from Army records, and those gave us the names of the rest. None of them say there was anybody who hated him enough to kill him, and in an outfit like the Army that sort of thing gets around. He didn't rob anybody, he didn't take anybody's woman, and he didn't make a habit of shooting unarmed civilians. Can I ask what you're grinning about, Mr. Blue?"

Blue nodded. "That German eighty-eight-millimeter gun. I never did believe in it, and I'm delighted to hear that it has been put away at last."

I protested to Sandoz, "But you were the one who said it was an artillery shell!"

"I did, Miss Hollander, and it was. After I'd wasted a lot of good men's time looking for the spot it had been fired from, I finally got it through my head that there's a big difference between a common bullet—that reminds me of something I forgot, by the way, and I'll get back to it—and a shell. A bullet has to be fired. Otherwise, it's just a little hunk of lead that can't hurt anybody. A shell doesn't. It can blow up, even if it's never seen the inside of a gun barrel.

"Let's suppose, Miss Hollander, that somebody had a shell like that. Maybe he stole it from a museum, or maybe he just found it lying around somewhere. If he was a clever man with tools, it would be pretty easy to rig up a way to detonate it, probably with a dynamite cap—they aren't hard to come by. If he wanted to be extra sure, he might even stick a little dab of some other explosive—gelignite, let's say—between the cap and the shell. I called up the Hollander Safe and Lock plant down in Indiana, and do you know, they use dynamite caps in their lab down there, and gelignite, too, to see how hard a safecracker would have to work to get into one of their new models."

"If my father had done what you're saying, and if he has all this stuff in his company—I'm not going to believe that just because you said it—he wouldn't have needed the shell at all."

"That's right, he wouldn't have. He could have used plain gelignite and the cap. But that way he couldn't have thrown us off with war stories. The way he did it, making the phone calls and using the shell, he had us chasing our tails. Probably he hoped we'd chase them forever—anyhow, that's what I

134

think now. Once I search this house, maybe I'll know better."

My father asked, "Are you finished?"

"Why no, Mr. Hollander. I haven't even said most of what I wanted to. Mostly I've been answering your questions, and your daughter's." Sandoz swiveled a little in the desk chair.

"I was talking about looking for connections, you remember, and I showed why it was I thought the murder of your brother was no mistake. What I mean to say is that whoever killed him meant to kill him, and not somebody else, or just anybody. So I asked myself if there was some similarity, some connection, to hook up that killing with the ones at the high school. It surely looked like the person who was intended to die there was Lawrence Lief, because of the calls. I got that information from your daughter, and I thank her for it. Those calls were meant, maybe, to throw us off; but *she* didn't mean to, I believe. She passed along her information in all innocence, and in the end it helped me quite a bit, because it eliminated that Munroe fellow. I didn't have to worry about him anymore.

"All the same, there didn't seem to be a connection between Lief and your brother. Naturally I thought of Miss Hollander, because she'd been hurt, too. But the bomb— I'm going to call it a bomb from here on—didn't seem like it was meant for her. Her being wounded was kind of a freak, and Mr. Blue here, who was talking to her when it went off, wasn't hurt at all. Just the same, she'd been there in that hospital and she was Herbert Hollander's niece. There was no getting around that.

"About the same time I gave up on the cannon idea, it hit me that maybe the bomb was intended for somebody in addition to Lief—somebody who'd link up Lief and Herbert Hollander, if only I could figure out who it was. Whoever made the bomb knew that Lief would be the one to open the box. That had been announced. It wasn't likely he knew

Drexel Munroe would be on the platform with him, although it was possible, as I explained once to Miss Hollander. But he might have *thought* that somebody else would be on hand—somebody who really wasn't there, and so didn't get hurt. Who might that be?"

Sandoz stopped talking for a minute and looked around at my father and Aladdin Blue and me. His face was just as wooden as ever, but there were red sparks in his eyes; he could have been the Indian who scalped Custer. "Why, Mrs. Hollander, of course. She'd been up on that platform just a short time before, for the drawing. She'd only gotten down because with her and Munroe and Lief up there, there wasn't room for Lief to work. If somebody hadn't known how big the platform would be—for instance, if he was in New York building himself a good alibi when it was put up—he'd think she'd be up there sure. She was a woman, wasn't she, and curious? He'd figure she'd stay there to see what was inside when Lief opened it."

My father said, "All this is speculation." His cigar had gone out, but I don't think he knew it.

"Sure it is," Sandoz admitted, "but look how good it hangs together, when nothing else will hang together at all. And we do have some evidence now, Mr. Hollander, which I'll show to you in a minute.

"So Lief was killed and your brother was killed and maybe Mrs. Elaine Hollander was meant to get killed. And that box was right here in this room for almost a month before it went into the window at the First National. So far, so good.

"Miss Hollander here knew Lief, and Mrs. Elaine Hollander was her mother, and Herbert Hollander was her uncle. But why would she want to kill them? I hear she doesn't get along with her mother too well, but that isn't much of a reason. I didn't think she could've picked the lock on that box, and I was pretty sure she couldn't have rigged up a dynamite cap to set off an artillery shell, even if she could get hold of one. And on top of that, Mrs. Lief, and Megan Lief, who as you may or may not know was Lief's sister, and old Mr. Lief, his father, all say that whoever made those calls about Vietnam was a man.

"That left you, Mr. Hollander. You've been the president of your company for nearly twenty years, and you don't look to me like a man who'd hold down a job like that without learning everything there is to know about the business. In fact, some people I've talked to have told me you made a hobby of it, and since I've been here in your den I've been looking at the titles of your books, and I can see that they're right. You could've gotten that box open before Lief did, and you could've rigged up a dynamite cap to set off an old artillery shell. Am I wrong?"

My father said, "You advised me that I was not required to reply to your questions. I don't believe I'll answer that one, Lieutenant."

"I don't blame you. In your position I don't think I would either. But I'm not quite done yet. If what I've said fits the facts like I think it does, then there were three people meant to die. You must've known that others would be killed when your bomb went off, but it was those three you were after— two with the bomb, and one later. Those three were Lief, who you knew would be the one to open the box, your wife, who you thought would be standing right beside him when he opened it, and your brother—that's the second assumption I mentioned a while back."

"I had no reason to kill any of those people." My father got out of his chair to get the big gold lighter from his desk and light his cigar again. You could see it had been a shock; but he was over it, fighting mad and cool as ice. I was proud of him.

"I think I can establish that you did, Mr. Hollander. Lief and your wife I'll leave aside for a minute—I think that one's pretty obvious anyway. To me the interesting one's your brother Herbert, although it's outside my jurisdiction.

All these years you've been the head of your company, only you didn't really own it at all. You see, we've checked around, and the majority of Hollander Safe and Lock's stock belonged to your brother: fifty-two percent. It was held in trust for him by a court-appointed guardian, and that guardian was you. For years it must have seemed like there wasn't any difference between you owning that stock and him owning it. You voted it for him and used part of the dividends to pay his bills at a fancy sanatorium, and banked the rest in the trust account. Sooner or later he'd kick off, and since he didn't have a will and couldn't make one that would stand up, why, as a matter of course the court would hand over everything to you, the brother who'd looked after him so well for such a long time.

"Then, right around the time you must've decided you were going to pay back Lief and your wife for what they'd been doing to you, your brother went over the wall. At first you must've hoped that in a few hours they'd have him back. Then it was in a few days. Then you must've hoped that he was dead somewhere, because you realized how dangerous to you and your position he was on the outside. I don't know if he was really crazy or not, and I doubt if you do yourself. But he was sane enough, like I said a while back, that he could pass on the street and even talk to people. All he had to do was get hold of some hungry lawyer and tell his story. It's one thing to keep a man in an asylum, and it's another one, a hell of a lot different, to get him back in there once he's on the outside and has some shyster to go to bat for him. You can just bet half the lawyers on Wacker would jump at the chance to represent somebody with that good a claim on fifty-two percent of Hollander Safe and Lock. They'd take his case on spec, hell yes they would, and loan him enough to get along on until it was settled."

"You said you had some hard evidence. I want to see it."

"Right now, Mr. Hollander," Sandoz said.

He leaned back in the desk chair then as if he was tired.

It hadn't ever occurred to me that even a wooden man might get tired, but I suppose they do. Sandoz looked like he'd spent a long day hunting buffalo as he reached into his coat and pulled out three little envelopes. One was pink, one yellow, one blue.

"What I need you to understand, Mr. Hollander, is that the game's over. Or that it's changed into a different game, if you want to put it that way. It's not a question of fooling us cops anymore. You lost that one. Now it's up to your lawyer, and with your money you can afford a good one. Maybe you can make them think you were crazy, like your brother did. Even if you can't, you won't fry. You won't even go to a maximum security prison like Pontiac. An executive like you? Prison won't be much worse for you than what your brother had in that asylum."

"I want to see what you have there," my father said. "Those envelopes."

"You have to understand that it's over with," Sandoz said again. "I know how it is—it must have been sitting on your chest ever since those two men died at the high school. Now's the time to get it off. You probably think we're your enemies, but we're not. We're just doing the job we're paid to do, and as far as we're concerned, as soon as you confess, it'll be all over."

"Damn it, what have you got there!"

Sandoz sighed and leaned forward. "Love letters," he said. "Undated except for the postmarks, but two of those can be read, and they're pretty fresh. They were written to Lief by a woman who signs herself 'Your Elaine.' She refers in one of them to her husband, and she calls him Harry. I understand that's what your family calls you."

"I don't believe you."

"They're real. Old Mr. Lief was going through his son's clothes; he was planning on giving them to the Salvation Army. He found these in the pocket of a winter shirt in the back of his closet. Lief didn't want his wife to come across them, I suppose. I can't let you handle them, but you can look at the writing." He held the pink envelope out so my father could see the address. "You know her handwriting, I would think. There must be plenty of samples around."

"I want to see the text of those letters."

"You'll hear them in court. If I was to read them to you now, the D.A. would have my hide. I wouldn't do it anyway, with your daughter here." Sandoz put them back in his pocket. "You wanted to know what we had. Well, that's what we have, and I believe a judge will think it's good enough for a warrant."

He paused and looked at each of us in turn. "Now let me think. I believe that's almost everything, except about the shooting—I said I'd get back to that. We were talking, you'll remember, about hit men. It was what we call a red herring, but I drug it in myself because I wondered if maybe you'd hired one to do the job on your brother, and I wanted to see how you acted when I talked about one. But I was going to say I didn't think it had been a hit man, because they hardly ever shoot just once. They know, you see, how hard it is to kill a man with a pistol. Why, just a few years ago there was that man down south that puts out the skin magazine. The guy who shot him did the job with a forty-four magnum, a gun that would snuff a grizzly bear, and he lived through it.

"Now I want to show you folks something. Mind if I borrow a pencil?"

Before my father could stop him, Sandoz pulled open the upper right-hand drawer of the desk and rummaged in it. When his hand came out again, he was holding a black automatic.

"I'd imagine," he said, "that we'll find this is the gun that killed your brother Herbert. You looked a little funny, Mr. Hollander, when I used the phone on this desk, so I thought I might find something. Is this it?"

"Of course not!"

140

I piped up. "I've seen that gun—it's been in there for years. It's not even a thirty-eight."

My father gave me a look that made me feel good all over. "That's right," he said. "Bert was shot with a thirty-eight, wasn't he? A policeman's gun. That one's a nine-millimeter; I brought it back from Germany. It even has Nazi markings."

"Sure," Sandoz said, holding the gun under the desk light. "Nine-millimeter *Kurz*. Somebody told me once that *kurz* means 'short' in German. Here in America we call that cartridge a three-eighty ACP—that stands for Automatic Colt Pistol—or a thirty-eight short. Same cartridge that killed your brother."

My father put his face in his hands.

18

How I Bailed Out

THAT much I've given you blow-by-blow because I think
you ought to have it, but I'm going to spare you a lot of
the rest. Just a few minutes after Lieutenant Sandoz pulled
the gun out of my father's desk, another cop came in
with the search warrant, and he and Sandoz and the one
called Jake started really searching in earnest. Up in Elaine's
bedroom they found a box of mix-and-match stationery—
pink, yellow, and blue, just like the letters Mr. Lief had
found. Also green, which I guess she hadn't gotten around
to using yet.

You know, people are crazy, and I mean particularly me.
It hadn't really come home to me when Sandoz showed those
letters to my father, but it did when Jake came pounding
down the front stairs with that box of stationery. It wasn't
even good stuff, just cheap writing paper like you might buy
in the Ben Franklin in Barton for maybe a buck seventy-
five; and it meant Elaine and Larry had been checking into
motels, or maybe doing it in the back of Larry's van or on

142

that couch in our basement. It made me feel sick; I thought about my father and how he was nuts over Elaine and had been for as long as I could remember, and about Molly and how she was nuts over Larry and believed he was this untarnished knight or something. I hated Elaine then. I hated her for being such a lightweight, so damned good-looking with nothing inside to back it up. I hated her for being my mother, and I hated her for marrying my father. If she'd just let him set her up in an apartment someplace and give her fur coats and diamond bracelets, I wouldn't have been where I was or anywhere, and that would have been just fine with me.

I think this is one of the things real, pro mystery writers aren't supposed to say, but I'm going to say it anyhow, and I learned it that day: murderers aren't any different from you and me. If I ever get really, really mad or really, really greedy, and especially if I get both together, I could murder somebody. So could you. That day, if somebody had tossed me that little Nazi automatic I could have knocked off Elaine when she walked through the door into the study. Which she did.

I was watching her like a hawk—a hawk with a broken wing. When she found out what was going on she turned pink under her powder, and then white; and when she caught on that they were just damned near certain to arrest my father, she fell on her knees and got him by the legs and said, "I'm sorry, Harry! I'm sorry, I'm sorry!" over and over again until Mrs. Maas came and got her on her feet again and led her away, I guess to lie down somewhere. Just about then Jake came down again, and this time he had two letters from Larry to Elaine. He said they had been under a jewelry box in her vanity.

Sandoz showed them to my father. "Is this how you knew? Did you find them before we did?"

My father shook his head, but he wouldn't say anything.

And that was about it. Naturally I was stuck on that sofa and couldn't see anything except what went on in the study. At the time that didn't bother me, but afterward I wished I could have gone around and watched. It might have been interesting. I know that the other cop, the one that had brought the warrant, spent a lot of time in my father's shop; and Sandoz spent a lot there in the study, reading papers and even pulling down books and riffling the pages; but the only funny thing he found wasn't a slip of paper, or even what you could call small. He got down on his knees with a penlight and looked under my sofa, and then stuck his arm in, and what he pulled out was a couple of round, black iron weights with handles on the top. They didn't seem to mean anything, and after he'd looked at them he pushed them back again.

When the cops were finished and the whole place was a mess, Sandoz went over to my father, coughed, and said, "You are under arrest, Mr. Hollander. Before we ask you any questions, you must understand what your rights are. You have the right to remain silent. You are not required to say anything to us at any time or to answer any questions. Anything you say can be used against you in court. You have the right to talk to a lawyer, and to have him with you during questioning. If you cannot afford a lawyer and want one—" (So help me, he said that.) "—a lawyer will be provided for you. If you want to answer questions without a lawyer, you still have the right to stop at any time. You also have the right to stop answering at any time until you talk to a lawyer."

After that, my father and the three cops went away. They didn't put handcuffs on him, but maybe I would have felt better if they had.

When we heard the front door close, Blue stood up and gave me his handkerchief. I'd been using the hem of my nightie, and I guess it was getting pretty wet. Blue's handkerchief was just a cheap cotton job that had been washed a lot, but it was clean. When I'd gotten calmed down a little I asked if he still had my father's check in his pocket.

"No," he said. "I have a Hollander Safe and Lock Company check, signed by the chief operating officer of the Hollander Safe and Lock Company."

"It's his check, and you know it. Couldn't you have done *something?*"

"I did what I could," Blue said.

"Like hell."

"No, Holly. What would you have wanted me to do? Argue in his behalf? As soon as I began, Sandoz would have forced me to leave—if necessary by having one of his subordinates arrest me on some trivial charge. As it was, he permitted me to remain. Most policemen originally became policemen because of a desire to show off—to strut in uniform, gun on hip. Most never quite outgrow it, and occasionally that can be employed to advantage. Lieutenant Sandoz wanted me, the criminologist, to realize what a clever detective he is."

"So now you do."

"Thanks to my silence, I know the case against your father, yes."

"Do you think he killed Larry and all those people?"

"Do you?"

I shook my head.

"Are you sure, or are you just being loyal to him?"

"I wouldn't be very loyal, would I, if I said I wasn't sure."

"As for me, I'm not certain what I believe." Blue stood up again, lifting himself on his cane the way he always did. "When I entered this room, I was, I admit—or almost certain, at least. That was the real reason I asked for a company check. It would have been less than ethical for me to have accepted a retainer from your father, as an individual, when I strongly suspected he had built that bomb. I was even more suspicious when he agreed to such a large one. Now I don't know."

"Wait a minute," I said. "That was before Sandoz showed us those love letters. In fact, it was before he ever came in and started his song and dance."

"Of course."

I wiped my nose. "So what made you think my father was the one? Had you figured out all that stuff Sandoz told us?"

Blue looked mad. "I'd thought of most of it, and rejected a lot of it. It had nothing to do with my decision. Look at the mantel over that fireplace and tell me what you see there."

"A picture of Elaine; a picture of my father and Elaine— you don't want me to describe the clothes in those pictures, do you? A map. That's on the rocks behind the mantel, really—"

"A map of what?"

"A map of Europe, with a red line from Italy to France and up into Germany, the way my father went. A German officer's hat that he makes Mrs. Maas clean with one of the attachments to the vacuum cleaner. Oh, and a fancy dagger. You don't notice that because it lies down flat. Was that what you wanted?"

"Specifically, a Nazi SS dagger; its blade is engraved with the rather fatuous sentiment, '*Meine Ehre heist treue*'—my honor commands me to be faithful. The Germans who fought for Hitler felt they were defending the right, difficult though that is for us to appreciate."

I said, "I don't understand why the dagger's important."

"It isn't. Or then again, perhaps it is, depending on how one looks at these things. You might say that it's no more and no less significant than the cap. Lieutenant Sandoz laid stress on the importance of similarities in solving seemingly unrelated crimes. Perhaps he should have considered that both the shell that exploded at the high school and the pistol he found in your father's desk came from Germany, and in fact from Nazi Germany."

"You didn't know about the pistol when you came in here. Or did you?"

Blue shook his head. "But I knew about the shell, so when I saw the officer's cap I crossed the room to have a look at it while your father was getting you settled on that sofa. I saw the SS dagger then, and I saw something else as well. You must have been in this room many times. Haven't you noticed by now that something's missing from the mantel?"

"No, I've never paid that much attention to that stuff."

"You're protecting your father, so I can hardly expect you to tell me; but that mantel shows quite clearly where the shell was removed from it."

"Are you talking about dust? I came in here one time and saw where Pandora's Box had been sitting on the library table, because Mrs. Maas hadn't dusted it yet. Only if you think she hasn't dusted in here since the bomb went off, you're batty. If that was true, I'd see dust all over, and I don't."

"That's not what I mean," Blue said. "It seems clear that your father telephoned and notified his family that he would be returning from New York—he would have to do it if he wanted to be sure his chauffeur would be free to meet him at the airport. When the word came, your Mrs. Maas would have taken good care to clean this room, as she obviously has. But when an object rests for years in one position on dark wood, the wood beneath it will always be darker than that around it; it has been protected from the light, which bleaches the exposed surface to some extent. A good deal of sunlight presumably comes through that large window for ten hours or more on many days. Eighty-eight millimeters is approximately three and half inches, which is what I estimated the dark spot at the end of the mantel to be. A man's thumb is roughly an inch across, in case you didn't know, and that fact is sometimes—please excuse the expression— a handy one."

147

"This doesn't mean a thing to you, does it? Just a cute little problem."

Blue sighed and leaned a little more weight on his cane; I got the feeling that his leg was bothering him. "Certainly it doesn't mean as much to me as it does to you. One of the things we all have to learn eventually is that our personal problems are not the personal problems of others. But I like you, and I don't want to see you hurt. Also, I'd like to earn the check in my pocket; I need the money badly, and though I'll deposit this as soon as I can and use the funds to stave off the worst of my financial difficulties, I probably won't see any more unless I earn it. If I sound facetious, it's because I'm not doing very well, and I must try, at times, to keep my own spirits up."

"You're a regular wizard," I told him bitterly. "With you on the case my father'll hang in a week."

"Although this state has restored the death penalty," Blue said, "it does the job by electrocution. For practical purposes, however, your father's risk of execution is nil, as Lieutenant Sandoz pointed out. Wealthy, middle-aged white men do not go to the chair." Blue limped over to the door. "Now I must be on my way. I wish that I could carry you back up to your room, but I can't. If you like, I'll ask Mrs. Maas to send the chauffeur in to you before I go."

"Mr. Blue—"

He stopped and looked back at me.

"Take me with."

"Are you serious?"

"Only for a couple of hours. Until dinner, okay? Then I'll go home, I promise. I have to get away from her."

"Your mother?" Blue was staring at me like he was trying to look right through me.

"As long as I was bitching at you it was all right, then when you went to leave it wiped me out. I'm going to have to be here with her, and every time I see her or hear her talking I'm going to think about what she did with Larry and what she did to my father—I need a little time to get my head straight. Please? She won't even notice, and if she does she won't give a damn." All of a sudden I understood, or thought I did, why Elaine had never cared about me, and I added, "I'm like him."

"You can't go dressed as you are."

"In the closet up in my room, you'll find about a dozen blue shirts and three or four wraparound jean skirts. Bring one of each."

"That's all you'll need?"

"That's all I could get on. Underpants wouldn't go over the bandages and stuff. Bring a bandanna, too, please. Top dresser drawer, right side. I'd better have a bandanna."

I sat there and listened to him thump up the stairs, and about five minutes later thump back down.

19
How I Was Entertained at Blue's

So there I was, sitting beside Blue in his old Rambler, my bad leg stuck straight out in front of me, holding on to my aluminum crutches. "What a beater!" I said.

And he said, "She's got almost two hundred thousand miles on her, and she still runs like a top."

Well, it takes all kinds.

The upholstery was shot, and I got the feeling that every time we hit a pothole we left behind a little red cloud of body rust; but once you realized that most of the racket was coming from a hole in the pipe, the engine didn't sound so bad. It was a regular three-on-the-tree automatic, so Blue could prop *his* bum leg up on the doghouse and drive with his good one. Seeing him do it made me wonder if I could do the same thing. I said, "Hey, what has two heads, four arms, and two legs?"

He had been thinking and gave me a Look, but after a minute he said, "You must be feeling better. I give up. What?"

"Us."

"Do you know the riddle of the sphinx? That would make it five."

"I'm afraid I don't. I ought to read more mythology, I guess."

Blue was quiet then until we'd left the private road and got almost to Barton. Then he said, "So should I."

"I thought you did already. A lot."

"Not as much as I should. Do you know, I left behind those books I bought at the book sale? I'd paid you for them, hadn't I?"

"I don't suppose there's much chance of getting them now."

"No. Fortunately, I read them first. Or at least, I read the parts I was most interested in."

We swung right at the corner of Main and Half, then veered off onto Barton Road past the Cow House (which is a big, fancy restaurant), and a couple of car dealers. On the other side of the nature preserve we swung onto a side road, then onto another and *then* onto another, with the land getting hillier and hillier all the way. Most of it was covered with thick woods; I suppose those trees had been cut down once to let cattle graze, but the last guy to cut them had probably never seen a car. Pretty soon we were off pavement altogether, jolting along a double strip of dust.

"You ought to get a Jeep," I told Blue.

"It's going to take quite a few more five-thousand-dollar checks before I'm able to think about that," he said. "But I want you to notice we have a private road, too."

"And a country place."

"Yes. Actually, it's amazing how much of the life of the rich is merely a glamourized counterfeit of the life of the poor. Did you know that penthouses were originally built to house the janitors who cleaned the buildings upon which they stood? That was in the days before elevators. The richest people lived on the ground floor so they didn't have to climb stairs."

We went around a sharp curve too fast, then down into a dark little gulch, then, all of a sudden, out of the trees and into a sunny clearing.

An old, old farmhouse stood there, with hollyhocks around it and purple morning glories climbing up the front porch. The house was two stories high, with turrets that didn't match and a steep roof that was green with moss; the rest had been white once, but so much paint was gone that it was pale gray.

"I bet it's haunted," I said.

"It is," Blue admitted as he climbed out of the car. "If you were to stay overnight, we'd find out whether the ghosts liked you. They're rather a nice crowd, really. Good country people."

"Dead country people." I wasn't sure he was kidding me.

"Aren't we all." He helped me get out, and I thought of the time I'd helped him get up into the CW&N car. A guy about twenty, with a tangled beard and hair to match, was standing in the doorway like he was waiting for us. I didn't know his name, but I remembered having seen him around Barton. "This is Muddy Brooks," Blue said. "Muddy, this is Holly."

Muddy nodded and smiled; he'd lost a couple of teeth. I looked at Blue, and Blue said, "Mrs. Maas. Muddy does most of our cooking and keeps the place swept out."

"I see."

"Muddy, Holly will be here until about dark. Do we have anything to eat?"

"Bread," Muddy said. "I baked today. Coffee. There's some of that apple butter left, and I could check the snares."

"Do it, please, and ask Tick to bring in some firewood, if you see him. We'll have a fire tonight."

We went on into what I guess had been the parlor in the old days. It was a big room with windows pretty near solid around two sides, so that there was a lot of light in spite of the morning glories. There was a fireplace in it with lots of

152

ashes, an old flattop desk that might have been a teacher's once, with a radio on it and a swivel chair behind it, and about six other chairs; as far as I could see, the swivel was the only chair that wasn't busted some way. Blue put me in a nice carved-oak morris that was perfectly okay except that the cushions didn't belong to it and the stick that was supposed to let you move the back up and down was gone and a three-foot piece of copper tubing was doing the job instead.

"Do you want your foot up on something?" Blue asked.

"Yeah," I said. "That would be great."

He shoved over a green plastic hassock that had sprung a leak, and Muddy came in carrying chipped white mugs that looked like they'd been ripped off from a diner. The coffee was hot and black, very strong and very, very bad.

"You said you wanted to get your head straight," Blue told me. "Is there anything I can do to help?"

"Listen, I guess, if I feel like talking."

"I can't stay around—I have errands to run. I'll be back this evening, though, and I'll listen then. All right?"

"All right."

"You'll be safe here; I don't want you worry about that. If you need anything, yell. Muddy or Tick will get it if we have it."

"All right," I said again. "Who's Tick?"

"Tick is Bill. He's crabby, but don't worry about it. You won't be able to make friends with him, so don't bother to try; but his meanness is all talk, and he doesn't talk much."

"These guys work for you? Tick and Muddy?"

Blue shrugged. "You can put it that way if you want. Or you could just say they live with me; legally I own this place, and a lot of the Hollander Safe and Lock Company's five thousand is going to take care of back taxes on it. Or you can say we're a commune of three; when you don't have money, it doesn't matter what your economic system is. Now I have to go."

Only he didn't—at least, not right away. He went farther

back in the house somewhere. I could hear, faintly but clearly (because that house was one of the quietest places I've ever been in), his dialing a phone. I couldn't make out what he said; there was another phone over on the flattop desk, and I had to fight the temptation to hobble over and listen.

After a while he came back, and I asked, "Something you didn't want me to hear?"

Blue shook his head. "When I deal with people, I'm often forced to promise that what they say—even their communicating with me at all—will be held confidential. I try to keep that promise."

"That's what I said," I told him, but I had to say it to his back.

After that I sat and thought. Outside you could hear the wind in the trees maybe once every five minutes, but that was all. There was somebody else in the house moving around, mostly upstairs, but there was nothing scary about it—he sounded like he must have been working because he moved too much for loafing, but it wasn't restless pacing up and down either, just somebody walking when he needed to get something. Eventually I heard him come downstairs for maybe the third or fourth time, and he stuck his head in to look at me. He stayed long enough to let me ask for something if I wanted it, and when I didn't he went away; he had been a big fat sour-faced man who wore moleskin work pants, construction boots, and no shirt.

When things are bad, I always figure that if only I could spend all day thinking about them I could get them straightened out in my mind. But when I really have the time—like then—either I find out it doesn't take nearly that long, or I just can't do anything with them and they chase their tails through my brain until they wear me out. This time it was the second one, and finally I knew I'd have to find something else to do or go nuts, so I got up on my crutches and started poking around.

HOW I WAS ENTERTAINED AT BLUE'S

Blue's desk had a file drawer, and the folders were full of letters. The first one that I read was from somebody who'd been in the slammer with him (black by the sound of it, although you couldn't be sure) who wanted help when he got outside. The next was from a woman who was answering some kind of ad he'd run and wanted to know if a criminologist could talk sense into her son. The third was from a woman he must not have been seeing anymore who wanted him back. I didn't know any of the people, and after the last one I got ashamed of what I was doing and stopped.

The drawer above had a little good white bond paper and a lot of cheap yellow paper, a supply of business cards like the one he'd given me on the train, the Greater Chicago White Pages, and a pencil that somebody had chewed. When I saw the paper, I remembered the letter somebody had sent to the *Trib;* but it had been done on an electric typewriter, and an electric typewriter wouldn't have fit in here. Anyway, there wasn't any. The flat drawer in the middle had more pencils, a couple of Bics, rubber bands, and some other junk.

The next drawer was the upper right, and that was where my father had kept that little Gestapo gun in *his* desk. It had hit me already how much this was like his study at home—I couldn't have missed it after what Blue had said in the car—and I was a little scared of what I'd find there. I'd already noticed Blue was a lefty (his watch was on his right wrist, which practically advertised it) but just the same . . .

I could have saved my sweat. A box half full of tapes for one of those little minirecorders, a booze bottle half full of milky stuff that was probably moonshine, and—I am not kidding—a magnifying glass. The lens was in a solid brass frame that looked old enough to qualify for the Barton Antique Fair and Art Festival easy, and I tried to think of something witty along the lines of the difference between rich people and poor people was that rich people had new

155

glasses and old whisky, but *magnifying* was too long and kept screwing it up.

Just one drawer left, and it was full of big envelopes, a lot of them recycled junk mail; they had clippings inside, and they weren't labeled, so I couldn't understand for the life of me how Blue knew what went where. I still can't. The top one had two pieces on diet (maybe for the fat man, Tick?), one on the social difficulties of obese women, one about the cigarette industry, and one about a guy who stuck radio telltales on sea turtles. Nuts.

There were bookcases made of boards and bricks, and others made out of crates, the crates under the windows and the board-and-brick jobs up against the walls that didn't have any. Lots of criminology, lots of true crime, and a few mysteries. Great Literature with capital letters. Maugham, Mark Twain, and some other stuff I didn't know at all and couldn't place. I found myself a book about the Cincinnati Strangler, a guy I'd never heard of who pulled some cute capers like stealing a cab and answering the calls he heard from the cab company's dispatcher.

Blue and Muddy got back almost at the same time. Muddy had three rabbits and looked happy, and Blue looked just the way he always did. He didn't really have an expressionless face like Sandoz's, and with those blue eyes and the thin, straw-colored hair there wasn't anything Indian about him. Just the same, you could have lost a lot of money playing poker with him. I said, "How'd it go?" and he said, "All right," and I said, "Want to tell me about it?" and he said, "Not yet." And that was that.

Muddy went back to the kitchen and cut the rabbits up, and Tick came in and built a fire and then went out and cut green sticks for us to roast with. We had roast rabbit and bread and apple butter and coffee, and except for the coffee it was about the greatest meal I ever ate in my life; I can still remember it. Tick didn't eat much (surprising me quite a bit) and Blue hardly ate anything; but Muddy and I put away almost a rabbit apiece. Finally I asked Blue if he was trying to get my father off.

"I'm trying to find out who killed your uncle and Larry Lief," he said. "It's much the same thing."

"You don't think he did?"

He shook his head; but he wouldn't say anything else, and when we were through eating he took me out to his car and drove me home. Bill wasn't around and neither was Mrs. Maas, but Blue helped me on the stairs as much as he could, and I didn't really have much trouble, although it was slow. While I was undressing I could hear him going downstairs. When he got to the bottom he didn't go out, though. He went into my father's study, if I was guessing right from the sounds, and stayed there for maybe half an hour. Okay, I'd searched his desk, so I couldn't complain.

20

How We Mulled

IT felt funny for our house to be so empty and quiet. I hadn't really expected Elaine to come running to see if her little girl was okay, but I'd expected, at least, to hear her and Mrs. Maas stirring around. After a while it got spooky. I played records, and that should have helped; but it didn't because I could hear the silence behind them, if you know what I mean; and when each record was over there would be nothing except the *click, click* of the changer and the *flop* of the next one dropping into place. When my hi-fi had gone through the stack, I let it switch itself off; I read for a little and took the medicine that was supposed to stop my leg from hurting, and went to sleep.

A door shutting woke me up. Not the front door—the back. Then I heard Mrs. Maas walking around in the kitchen; I listened for two or three minutes, I guess, before I was sure it was her, and then, boy, did it ever sound good. I could have yelled or rung my bell for her to come up, but I didn't even think about it.

I switched on my light instead, grabbed my crutches and

got up. My little clock said it was after midnight, but I started downstairs, scared to death I'd fall because I couldn't use both crutches and hang on to the banister at the same time, but bound and determined to find some human company. I decided right then that if I ever get rich and build a house of my own it's going to have an elevator.

Mrs. Maas must have heard me, because she came and dithered and more or less helped me down the bottom half of the stairs. I don't think I've said a lot about Mrs. Maas so far, but maybe I ought to here. She was blond, a little bigger than average but not really big, solid-looking and muscular. I never asked how old she was, but her hair was starting to get gray and I'd say about fifty. One time she told me she had grown up on a farm, and both her parents had been born in the Old Country. She was a widow.

Here I'm going to psychoanalyze. If you don't like it (and in a lot of books I've read I don't) you can skip this bit. I think that while Mrs. Maas had been with us I had been trying, without really knowing what I was doing, to make her my mother. Or my grandmother or aunt—whatever. You know what I mean. And I think Mrs. Maas had been through it before someplace and had lost her job because somebody's real parents saw she was getting closer to their kid than they were.

Naturally I can't prove any of that; but that night we were both tired and scared, and we practically fell into each other's arms. She didn't say anything special to me, just, "Oh, Holly, my poor Holly!" and I didn't say anything special to her; but by the time she had helped me into one of the kitchen chairs and put on water to make cocoa, we both felt quite a bit better.

"Where have you been?" I said.

And she said, "Didn't they tell you? They took me away, down to the police."

"In Barton?"

"Yes, to Barton. Afterward they said if I would take the

lie test they would let me come home. I said yes, and we went to Constance." She showed me where they'd stuck the sensors on her. "They asked a million questions. Some two or three times, saying it different ways."

"What kind of questions?"

"About your father. Bill is still there, they were going to do him after."

"What'd you tell them?"

"That he is such a good man, only away too much. They asked if he had fights with your mother, and I said no."

"Mrs. Maas, that was a lie. The machine must have jumped the track."

"No, it was not a lie. Not real fights. In fights someone hits or throws. What your father and mother have are arguments. I don't think you ever in your life saw your mother with a black eye, Holly."

"Of course not."

"Not of course. I have seen my own mother with many black eyes."

"Were you afraid?" I meant when her father hit her mother, but she didn't understand.

"I was. Yes. Not for myself, because I knew they would let me go. For your father. And for me, too, because if they don't let him go there will be no place for me and I will have to pack, pack all my things and find a room to live in until the agency gets me a new position. All the time I will be thinking of you and your family and this house."

The kettle sang, and she went over to pour water for my cocoa, and then the kitchen door opened and there was Elaine in a negligee. "It's you two," she said. "How's your leg, Holly?" I don't think she knew I'd been gone.

I said, "Okay. The cops had Mrs. Maas."

"I know. They took Mrs. Maas and Bill. I think they would have taken me, too, if I hadn't been much too upset to tell them anything. After a while I swallowed four of my pills and went to sleep. I just woke up."

Mrs. Maas asked, "Would you like cocoa, Mrs. Hollander?"

"Yes," Elaine said. "I would. I'd like some cocoa." She got another chair and pulled it up to the table and sat, and I remember thinking it was probably the first time in her entire life that she'd ever sat down in that kitchen. Usually she only went in there if she had to give last-minute orders to Mrs. Maas or the caterers, and got out as fast as she could.

"When do you think we'll see Dad again?"

"Tomorrow, I suppose. Don't they let them out on bail?"

"I think so."

"Then they'll have to let him go on bail. I'll call Harvey Webber," (that was my father's lawyer) "and Harvey will get him out. But . . ."

"But what?" I asked.

"But, Holly, it won't be for terribly long—perhaps not for more than a few weeks. You have to realize that. Then there'll be the trial, and then he'll be gone."

"You think he did it?"

Elaine didn't answer. Mrs. Maas had brought her cocoa in a pedestal mug exactly like mine; but when she raised it to her lips ever so delicately and sipped like she was afraid it was too hot to drink, which it was, it seemed like hers might be the chalice from the palace holding the brew that was true. There are a lot of pretty women. I'm a pretty woman myself, and maybe Mrs. Maas was once, too, because she was tallish and a blonde, and she must have had a good complexion when she was younger. But Elaine was beautiful the way a sunrise is beautiful, or wild geese flying over you. When you saw her profile like that, not expecting it, it could make you catch your breath.

"What are we going to do?" I asked her finally.

"I don't know, Holly. I don't know how much money there will be."

"If there isn't much."

"We're not going to starve, I don't mean that. There'll be enough to keep us. But when I try to think about what I'll do, I find I'm only thinking about what I won't. You'll finish high school and go on to college, and after that, we'll see. I won't marry again, or live with some man. Harry wouldn't like it, and I wouldn't either."

I couldn't help thinking that if she'd felt more like that before, we wouldn't be in the mess we were in now; I suppose she saw it in my face.

"When you're older you'll understand, Holly—or you won't." She still wasn't looking at me, just out of the kitchen window. The ground there sloped down toward the stable, and it seemed to me Elaine was looking at the stars above the treetops. "Whether there's a great deal of money or just a little, we'll be able to do what we like, with nobody to say no. I'll have an apartment in New York or London. I'll go to plays, and . . ."

"You'll have to come back, if you want to visit Dad."

"I will, of course; I'll fly. And of course the business— I'll have a business manager here." Suddenly she turned to look at me and those big beautiful violet eyes just seemed to swallow me up. "You'll come to visit *me,* won't you, Holly? You'll have vacations and holidays. We can go shopping together, and if I'm in New York I'll take you to Sardi's or the Plaza for luncheon. We'll have such a good time."

"I won't come if you don't want me to."

"Oh, but I do! I'll want to see you, Holly, and we won't fight anymore. I know you don't believe me, but you'll see. We won't. All this awful pressure will be gone, no more living together when we don't like it and no more groveling for crumbs. What are you going do with your life when you're finished with college? Don't say get married. That isn't a life."

I had to think fast, because I really hadn't done a whole lot of planning. "Get a job on *Time,* maybe, or *The New Yorker.*" Elaine smiled and gave my hand a squeeze.

Bill still hadn't come back when I went up to bed, so I had to do it pretty much on my own. My leg hurt some—there wasn't any question but that it liked being up on the bed or something better than swinging in the air—but it wasn't more than I could take, and I was proud of myself for having done what I did.

The trouble was that I couldn't get back to sleep. I kept thinking about everything that had happened, about what Sandoz had said in my father's study before he took him away, and about going to Blue's, and then about Blue and me and my father, then about how Sandoz had come in and everything he'd said, and so on and so forth, around and around. Eventually I got clear back to the day the bomb went off, and even the day that I met Blue when I went out to visit Uncle Herbert. That was when I decided that sooner or later I'd write this book; and I began to write it in my head there in bed that night. Believe me, I was a lot more anxious to see how it came out than you are.

Sometimes when I find a really good mystery, I stop reading a little before the end and go over the whole first part two or three times, underlining the stuff I think might be significant. Then, if the author's played fair, pretty often I can guess how it's going to end. So I did it that night, and the underlined parts of my memory are the parts I've written down here. That night I tried to solve it, just like I try to solve the books; but I came up against a couple things that bothered me. I think it's only fair to tell you about them now.

In the first place, in a lot of books I've read there are only a certain number of people who could have done it, usually fewer than ten. They're all in a big house in the country, or maybe on a ship—something like that. But what had happened to Larry and Mr. Munroe and Uncle Herbert and Mrs. Whoosis wasn't like that at all. The killer could be anybody in the whole wide world, and there was no guarantee whatsoever that the killer (I was sure then that it wasn't my father) who had set the bomb at Barton High had also killed Uncle Herbert. I think it would be awfully nice for the cops if they had more cases like the ones in books, where the murderer's got to be one of seven or eight people; but until somebody can arrange it, maybe we should have a law that says the murders in books have to be more like real ones.

Another thing was servants. In a book you can bet your booty it isn't old Portwine the butler, no matter how guilty he looks on page ninety-four; and I think the real reason for that is snobbishness. The murderer has to be somebody important, and somebody important can't be working class, a fact that would be big news to lots of union presidents. In real life, everybody knows it just isn't so; working-class people have killed plenty of other people, including quite a few very important ones. So it could be Bill or even Mrs. Maas; I didn't believe it, but I couldn't rule them out.

Okay, let's get down to cases.

The first big question was, where was the bomb? It seemed pretty likely that it had been in Pandora's Box, since the shell hadn't been fired (according to Sandoz) and a thing like that—an artillery shell—would have been pretty big and hard to hide. But if I allowed it was in the box, somebody must've gotten the box open and put it there, and the only people I could think of that I thought could have done it were my father and Larry. If it had been Larry, he wouldn't have done it and blown himself up unless he'd wanted to commit suicide.

Only come to think of it, it was possible he had, what with those mysterious calls and all. In a book, naturally, you could rule out suicide, but I couldn't. Maybe Larry had fixed up the bomb—getting the shell one of the times he came to see Elaine, and picking the lock and so on—just to kill himself. But if he had, we'd never prove it; and anyway, I couldn't really believe it.

That left Dad. I don't have to give the case against him,

because Sandoz already did; but what about the case for him? He could have picked the lock, sure. The box had been right there in his study for a couple of weeks at least (I couldn't remember just how long, but it was plenty of time) and so was the shell. Only if it was him it was all over and there was no use thinking about it. And anyway I couldn't believe that it was. Not just because he was my father and I loved him, but because a bomb at the Fair wouldn't have been his style. If he'd wanted to mess up Larry and Elaine, he could have done it a dozen ways without doing anything illegal or running any risk. For starters, how about tipping off Molly and filing for divorce, which he could have gotten with no alimony when he showed that Elaine had been unfaithful? He had money and lawyers and a sharp, cool brain. None of that fit with a bomb and risking the chair.

Which left me nothing but dark horses. Maybe, just maybe, Bill would have been able to pick that lock. He'd fixed things around our place and made some minor repairs on the cars. Who could say he might not be good with a lock? He could have been mad at Elaine because of something she said. Or if he knew, he could have wanted her himself and been jealous because Larry'd had her and he'd never get her. And come to think of it, it was damn near certain he had known; servants always know that stuff.

Or what about Aladdin Blue? All along I'd been ruling him out like he was the detective. Outside of a book, you can't do that. He'd been anxious to find out whether I knew what was in the box, and he'd been nice and far away when the bomb went off. As far as I knew, he'd never been to our house while the box was there; but it wasn't downright impossible that he'd gotten into it while it was in the window at the First National. I hadn't heard that anybody'd ever checked into how well they watched it, and one thing for sure is that a bank's window isn't the same as a bank vault— maybe you've noticed they don't put money in the window. Or maybe he'd gotten to the box while it was at the Fair;

after all, he was there. Nobody had ever proved that the shell that went off at Barton High was the same one that had been on our mantel. Germany must have made a million of those shells. When my father had carried me down the stairs, he'd been pretty careful, and even though Blue was lame he'd gotten ahead of us. My father had said, "To your left," and Blue had gone into the study before we did. Suppose that instead of *finding* that dark spot, he'd picked up the shell and hidden it so well that Sandoz hadn't found it when he searched the room. Then this evening, maybe, when Blue had gone in there, he'd fished it out and taken it away. Two things for sure about Blue: he was an ex-con, and he was slick enough to slide up a flagpole.

21
How I Joined the Investigation

PROBABLY everybody's done it. You go to sleep all in a dither, and you wake up knowing just what you ought to do. That was how it was with me. I don't mean I knew who done it, though if I'd had to vote right then I think I would have said Bill for Larry and some mugger for Uncle Herbert; but I knew what I personally, Holly Hollander, was going to do that very morning to try to get things squared away. I got up and got dressed, putting on the same clothes I'd worn the day before. It was before seven, and I figured that if I got going right away Mrs. Maas wouldn't be around yet. I scribbled a note for her: "Important Stuff. Back Soon. Thanks! Holly," and left it on the kitchen table. She kept the keys in the Ford in case the Caddy was laid up or off somewhere and Elaine needed it.

Let me come clean right here, so you don't get the wrong idea. I don't enjoy driving, and I'm not a very good driver. In fact, I nearly flunked driver's ed, and that's right next door to impossible. What's more, I was driving with the wrong leg, if you know what I mean. My good one wasn't used to the accelerator or the brake, and my bad one couldn't help. What was worse, I got to thinking that Blue must have gone through the same thing, learning over again after they'd shot him, and I almost put the Ford in the ditch. When I got it stopped and backed up onto the road, I sat there and shook for five minutes or so, and swore to myself that after that I'd keep my mind on my driving.

Only I couldn't, because I kept trying to figure out what I ought to do, and then what I ought to do if so-and-so happened, and then what I ought to do after that. And besides, I had to remember how to get to Blue's place, and trying to find it I got lost a couple of times, so it must have been after eight when I finally got there.

Even so, I'd been wondering if he'd be up yet; but when I pulled up in front of the house I got the surprise of my life—one of them, anyhow. Parked alongside Blue's rusty old Rumbler was a Chevy that was almost as old and almost as rusty, and it was a car I knew as well as ours: Uncle Dee's.

He came out the front door while I was still trying to make it up the steps, and I suppose he must have been just about as surprised to see me as I'd been to see his car; but he gave me a hand and one of his thousand-watt smiles and told me how good I looked and how he would have come to see me if he'd known I was out of the hospital. I shouldn't have broken down, I guess, but I did. I told him he'd have to be quick because I didn't know how much longer we'd be in our house. Then I started in on how they'd arrested my father, and before I knew what had happened I was bawling like two soap operas. Tick and Muddy came out then; Tick beat it back into the house, but Muddy stayed with me even after Uncle Dee had loaned me his handkerchief, whispered, "Now, now, Holly, I know all about it; believe me, Harry's going to be all right," and kissed me on the cheek and driven away. He left me his hanky, and I was glad, because I didn't have one and Muddy didn't look like he'd have a clean one.

"I've got to see Mr. Blue," I said.

"Sure, sure," Muddy told me, and led me inside.

Blue was in the kitchen with a mug of coffee and a bowl of some kind of breakfast cereal in front of him. There wasn't any milk on it, it was just the dry flakes, and it didn't look to me like he'd eaten any of it. There was another chair pulled up to the table, too, with a half-full coffee mug in front of it that must have been Uncle Dee's.

"I'm sorry," I said; I was still wiping my eyes.

Blue's head jerked, and he said, "Oh, Holly. What are you doing here?"

Muddy said, "He doesn't hear a thing when he's thinkin'. The stove could blow up." Then to Blue: "She was out in front cryin', Al. Me and Tick went out and got her."

Blue nodded as if that was just what he'd figured. "Sit down. How about some fresh coffee?"

I said thanks.

"Have you had breakfast, Holly? Muddy bought a few things yesterday. You can have this, if you want it. Muddy, did you get any cream?"

"Not unless you want some, too, Al."

Blue shook his head. "Oh, for God's sake!"

"He don't eat." Muddy was out for my support. "He wants to keep weight off his leg, but he's gonna kill himself." It can't have been easy for a guy not much older than me, sporting a scuzzy beard, to look righteous; but Muddy could have been a bishop.

I said, "No, I haven't eaten. I'd like some cereal with plain milk, if it isn't too much trouble."

"Milk for both of us," Blue said, giving up, "and how about some coffee for Holly?"

Muddy nodded happily. "I'll fry some bacon, too. I stole some."

"He means he got it cheaply," Blue said.

Muddy winked at me.

I got into the other chair and leaned my crutches against the table. "I guess you're wondering what I'm doing here, but first I'd like to know why Uncle Dee was."

"And I won't tell you," Blue said. "I want you to forget you saw him—for my sake, as well as his." He sounded serious.

"Like that, huh? Okay, I forget."

"I mean it. You came here for my help, I think. If you want it, you must forget you saw Sinclair and his car."

"Who said anything about Uncle Dee? I haven't seen him since before the bomb. How'd you know I wanted your help?"

"You came here. If you'd discovered something you thought might help, or simply wanted to know what I was doing, you would have telephoned; besides, you were crying when Muddy brought you in."

"That was because I ran into some guy whose name I forget when I wasn't expecting it. I guess you could say I want to consult you. I've got an idea I think might lead to something, and I want you to tell me whether you think it's a good one, and give me some advice on how to go about it. As for phoning, I'd think they'd have ours tapped by now."

Muddy plunked a bowl of cereal and a spoon in front of me, and poured milk over Blue's. I tasted mine: Wheaties.

"The courts have made legal taps very difficult for the police, but I'm glad you asked before doing anything. In fact, I'm glad you came."

"Great. Here's my pitch. Last night before I got to sleep I spent a lot of time going over everything that's happened. I picked and pulled at all the important stuff—Pandora's Box, for instance—and couldn't get a fingernail in. So what I think is that if you can't grab on to anything important, maybe you ought to get hold of something that isn't and give it good yank. Who knows, if I can start a long enough ravel some of the important stuff might come loose."

"No investigator would disagree with you."

"Goody. So here's my loose end. Tell me if it isn't worth doing, and if it *is,* give me some advice on how to do it."

"I'll try," Blue promised.

Muddy brought over a big plate of bacon. He must have fried the whole pound, and it was country style—soft and greasy—which happens to be the way I like it.

"My loose end's Molly. Remember when I was in the hospital and I told you and Sandoz about going to the Magic Key, and the phone calls for Larry? Later you told me you already knew about them."

Blue nodded.

"Then you probably remember how Megan told me that whenever this guy called he'd ask for Sergeant Lief, and when they said he wasn't there, he'd hang up. Megan said his voice was scary, but that's all he said."

"I remember, yes."

"Okay, here's the part I didn't tell. I didn't because the cop was there and I didn't want to get Molly in trouble. While we were talking, Molly pulled a gun from under the register and said if anybody hurt Larry she'd shoot them. It was a revolver, I think a thirty-eight, and after Uncle Herbert was shot I just kind of wondered if maybe Molly had decided he did it. But then yesterday Sandoz took that Gestapo gun of my father's—"

"It was a PPK," Blue interrupted. "Those letters stand for *Polizei Pistole Kriminal,* by which the Walther Corporation meant that it was intended for what we would call plain-clothes men."

"Yeah, that's what I said. So if he was right, it wasn't a revolver at all, which means it wasn't Molly."

"No," Blue said, "all it means is that if it was Molly who killed your uncle, she employed a weapon other than the one she showed you; but we have no better reasons to suspect Molly than several other people. And it was, in fact, a semiautomatic that fired the shot. The police have the bullet, and it is the fully jacketed type used in semiautomatics. Perhaps I should add that they also found the ejected brass, which is how Sandoz knew in what part of that parking lot your uncle died; revolvers don't eject their spent cartridges. I think we can safely assume that by this time they've run a ballistic comparison that will enable them to say for certain whether the pistol Sandoz took from your father's drawer killed your uncle. The results of that test are among the things I must determine this morning."

I waved all that aside. "What I'm trying to say is that Molly had a gun and was ready to *kill* whoever made those calls if Larry got hurt. Now I ask you—a guy keeps calling, asking for Sergeant Lief. Maybe he tells war stories—that's what I heard her say on TV one time. Does the way she was acting make sense? Maybe he did sound scary—some people just naturally do, and over the phone it might sound worse. Maybe he got shot in the throat or something in Vietnam."

"All right," Blue said, "Molly seems to have been overreacting. Go on from there."

"What I think is that whenever this guy—let's call him X, it sounds good—called and got Megan, he knew he had Larry's kid sister. He didn't want to scare her, or maybe just didn't think it was worth the trouble. But when he had Molly, he said more than she told the TV people about. Maybe she told the police, maybe not. Maybe she told you."

Blue shook his head.

"So that's my loose end. I want to try to get her to tell me everything he said, and especially why she thought it was so serious she pulled out that gun. Then we'll follow wherever it leads, and maybe it'll just peter out and maybe it won't. What I need for you to tell me is how to go about it."

"You're a woman," Blue said. "You were born knowing more about how to go about something of this sort than I'll ever be able to learn. But if I were you, I think I'd simply go to her in private and explain what it was that I wanted to ask and why I wanted to ask it. I would tell her that I loved my father, and that Larry cannot be hurt anymore—that he is forever out of harm's way. I'd begin by asking her to repeat the caller's exact words, as nearly as she remembers them; when she had done so—and not before—I would ask whether she had not, at least at some time, suspected that he was someone she knew."

"Okay, I'm going to give it my best shot."

"Fine." Blue was looking absentminded, and so help me he reached out and got a slice of bacon and ate it. I couldn't see Muddy from where I sat, but I was willing to bet he was jumping for joy. "However," Blue went on, "I think it would be best if you were home by, roughly, ten-thirty. Do you think you might manage that?"

I looked at my watch. "Sure."

"And it would be well for you to bring Molly. Particularly if she has told you what you want to know."

"To my house? What am I supposed to do with her when I get her there?"

"I'll be there as well," Blue said, "and I'll let you know then."

22

How Elaine Let the Cat Out of the Bag

MY bum-leg driving rattled Molly so much we had to stop halfway so I could slide over and she could walk around. After that her driving rattled me. She was one of those hay-wagon drivers who think the engine may bolt and jerk the wheel out of their hands. Also she liked to come to a complete stop before making a turn, which rattled the drivers in the cars behind us who didn't know her turn signal meant she was about to hit the brakes that hard. By the time we got to my place—I should really say my father's—I was ready to get out and walk, bum leg and all.

It was nearly a quarter to eleven, and Blue and Uncle Dee had beaten us. Their cars were out front, and they were in the living room talking to Elaine, Uncle Dee perched on the edge of his chair looking tense, Blue sitting about the way he usually did, with his hands on the handle of his stick.

"Oh, it's you, Holly," Elaine said. "You should be in bed." Uncle Dee and Blue stood up.

I performed introductions. "This is Mrs. Lief. She was Larry's wife." I honestly didn't know if Larry's father or the cops had told Molly about the letters yet. If the cops hadn't, they were bound to soon; but damned if I was going to do it and light a crisis. "Molly, this is my mother, Elaine. De Witte Sinclair. Aladdin Blue."

"We've met," Blue said. "Hello, Molly."

Uncle Dee said, "Charmed, Mrs. Lief," and inclined his head in a little bow.

Elaine had nothing to spare for Molly. "Holly, your friend Mr. Blue has already telephoned the police, he says. Now he's threatening to call the television news people. You know Jane Dalton had a television crew in her house about the garden tour, and she says it was terrible."

Uncle Dee said, "I don't believe they'll be coming, Elaine. At least, I hope not."

Since Elaine wouldn't offer her a seat, I put Molly on the sofa with me.

"I won't let them in," Elaine declared. "Not unless they tell me everything they intend to do first." Her purse was on the coffee table in front of her, and she got out her compact to check herself over for the cameras. "Does anyone know exactly how their makeup differs? Do they make up women, too, or is it just a matter of powdering the men?"

The chimes sang their little tune.

"Holly, could you—oh, no, of course you can't. I don't know where Mrs. Maas has gotten to. I hate to answer my own door. De Witte . . . ?"

Uncle Dee stood up again, which didn't take a lot of effort since he'd damn near been standing up when he was sitting down. "I'm not sure this is appropriate, Elaine, but since you asked."

He went out into the hall, and in a minute my father came in, with Sandoz in front of him and Jake and Uncle Dee behind him. No cuffs. Sandoz looked around at us, nodding to Elaine and Molly and me, and giving Blue a hard stare.

Blue said, "The gentleman who opened the door for you is De Witte Sinclair. Mr. Sinclair, Lieutenant Sandoz."

Sandoz nodded, not offering his hand and not bothering to introduce Jake.

My father asked, "May I sit down? I'd like the pleasure of sitting in my own house again."

"Sure," Sandoz said. "Go ahead." My father put one of the occasional chairs next to Elaine's, and she took his hand; Jake went over to stand beside him.

Elaine said, "I'm not certain I understand what's going on here."

"As far as we're concerned, it's not too complicated, Mrs. Hollander," Sandoz told her. "Mr. Blue there called me about an hour ago. On the phone he indicated he had positive proof that your husband is innocent. I told him then—and I'm telling him again now—that if that's the case, all he has to do is turn it over to me. He wouldn't come to our headquarters to discuss the matter, so we came here. If he's wasting our time, we'll soon find out. If he has what he says he has, we don't want to hold an innocent man any longer than necessary."

My father said, "You're ready to concede that I might be innocent? That's good of you."

Sandoz answered levelly, "Under the law, everyone's assumed innocent until a court finds him guilty, Mr. Hollander."

Blue lifted his stick to get their attention. "Perhaps I should explain. As Lieutenant Sandoz says, I called him this morning. I informed him that I had obtained a confession from the man who killed Larry Lief, Drexel K. Munroe, Edith Simmons, and Herbert Hollander the Third. I have—you'll hear it in a moment. I also told him that it would be necessary for him to come here and bring Mr. Hollander with him, and that if he refused I would hold a press conference without him or any other representative of Pool County present, a conference to which I would invite the news departments of the Chicago TV stations as well as reporters from the *Tribune*, the *Sun-Times*, and the *Daily Press*. I warned him that if he failed to cooperate with me, it was likely that Mr. Hollander would file suit for false arrest as soon as he was released, as he surely would be."

My father smiled. It seemed to me it was the first time I'd seen him smile in a long, long while. "You say the man's confessed?"

"I'll let you hear it for yourself," Blue said; and then he looked over at Uncle Dee, and I felt like the bottom had dropped out of the world.

Sandoz said, "I don't think I know you, Mr. Sinclair. Who are you?"

Uncle Dee cleared his throat. "I am a dealer in old and rare books. Mr. Hollander's one of my customers. He has been for years." He let it lie there.

"Go on."

"A detective, I suppose one of your men, came just once to talk to me. I wasn't at the Fair, you see—or rather I was, but I left early."

Sandoz said, "Just go ahead and tell it your own way." I felt like I was going nuts, but I could see he was right: keep 'em talking.

"I come to the Fair each year for the book sale. Several other dealers do as well, but I've priced the books myself and know exactly where the ones I wish to buy are located. I take what I want, pay, and leave; everyone knows I have no interest in antiques other than books. I realized, of course, that I'd be gone before my bomb went off."

Elaine whispered, "This is incredible."

Sandoz said, "I've got you placed now. Miss Hollander told us it was you that got her the cashiering job at the book sale."

"That's right." Uncle Dee looked at me, then looked away. "I like Holly, and I wanted her to be where she would be safe. I was wrong about that, she got hurt anyway, and I'm sorry."

Elaine, not whispering now, said, "De Witte, I can't let you do this!"

"I loved Elaine, you see, Lieutenant. She wouldn't have me, wouldn't let me touch her, but that was all right. She was a married woman, and I could understand and admire a lady who wouldn't betray her vows and her husband. Then I learned about Lief, and I thought I had a chance after all . . ."

I checked Molly out of the corner of my eye. She must have known already; she was taking it all right.

Sandoz said, "But you didn't?"

Uncle Dee shook his head. "She laughed at me. Elaine, you mocked me, and that was too much. I decided to kill you and to kill him, to kill you and your lover together."

Sandoz nodded like he had known all along. "So you put the bomb in the box. How'd you do that?"

"I came to this house often to show Harry books. One night when I knew that he and Elaine would be out, I came as though I had been invited. When the housekeeper told me they were gone, I said that Mr. Hollander was expecting me; she let me wait in his study, where we always talked. The box was there, on the table. I'd read about that type of lock in one of the books I'd found for Harry, and the tools I required were in the satchel in which I normally carry books. I picked the lock, and used the dud shell from his mantelpiece for the charge."

"You had the trigger mechanism with you?"

"That's correct. It was a simple affair, really—a small battery and an electrical switch I arranged so as to set off my blasting cap when the box was opened."

"You'd planned all along to use the shell?"

Uncle Dee nodded. "Harry had told me about it a couple of times. He had been a young corporal, a supply clerk, in Italy during the war. His outfit hit the beach, and just after he got off the LST that shell tossed sand in his face. He said he had thrown himself flat afterward, and that he must have

178

lain there a couple of minutes waiting for it to go off. Then he realized that if it hadn't been a dud he would have been killed already, and stood up and went away to do whatever it was he was supposed to be doing.

"A day or so later, when things had quieted down somewhat—am I telling this right, Harry?—he discovered that the chain on which he wore his dogtags had broken. He went looking for them and found them where he had thrown himself down that first time. That reminded him of the shell, and he dug it up to look at. It was a foolish thing to do because it might have exploded, but he said he had the feeling that since it hadn't gotten him when it had the chance, it never would."

Sandoz said, "So this time you decided to give it a little help. You must have known that it would be traced back to him eventually."

Uncle Dee nodded again. "He had her and Lief had her, but I couldn't; I was going to get them both. Harry had packed that shell in his company's supplies and trucked it all over Europe, that's what he told me. If it had done what it was supposed to do the first time, perhaps I would have found Elaine. This time I was going to make certain it didn't miss."

Very softly Blue inquired, "Do you want to tell them about Herbert Hollander now?"

"I suppose I'd better." Uncle Dee mopped his forehead; I could see his hand shake. "But first—Lieutenant, am I going to have to repeat all this again later?"

Sandoz nodded. "For a police stenographer, Mr. Sinclair. She'll type it up and you'll have to sign it."

"Then I'll try to keep it short. That same evening, when I put the bomb in the box, I got Harry's gun from his desk drawer. He had shown it to me about a year ago when there was a rash of home invasions here and I advised him to get a dog. He said he didn't need a dog, he had that, and showed me where he kept it. I thought that if either Elaine or Lief

escaped the bomb I'd use it to kill them, then put it someplace where it would be linked to him. I felt sure the servants
could identify it, and if they wouldn't, I'd do it myself.

"My bomb worked, as you know. I was certain it would;
I had tried out the mechanism with blasting caps several
times in advance." He glanced around at us when he said
that, his smile only a sickly imitation of his old one. "Blasting
caps aren't much more powerful than the big firecrackers—
salutes, they were called—that I used to shoot off as a boy.
I tested the battery and switch in my basement, and I doubt
that the people next door heard anything.

"So I was confident, you see—quite confident, when I
came here. Then I realized that I had forgotten the black
vinyl tape I had intended to use. I taped the cap to the shell
with Scotch tape from Harry's desk instead, and as it turned
out that worked just fine."

Sandoz said, "Except that Mrs. Hollander wasn't killed."

Uncle Dee had always had a clean handkerchief in his
breast pocket; now he was wadding it between his hands.
"That's right, she wasn't touched. She'd left the platform
before my bomb went off, and of course I couldn't kill her
afterward until Harry got back."

"But you had the gun."

"That's right. I carried it with me everywhere, because I
didn't know when Harry would come home and I'd have a
chance at Elaine. Something else had gone wrong as well,
however; Holly had been injured. As I said before, I'd tried
to arrange things so she wouldn't be. I felt that the least I
could do was visit her, bring her something to read in the
hospital."

"And you met Herbert Hollander in the parking lot?"

"Yes, and that destroyed my whole plan, or at least at
the time I thought it did."

"Why'd you kill him, Mr. Sinclair?"

"I had to. Several times when Harry couldn't come to see
about him, I had gone in his place, as his deputy so to speak.

180

Sometimes I'd taken Harry's check to the sanatorium, and once or twice when I thought Bert wasn't getting the treatment he should have had, I'd told Harry about it and relayed his instructions to the doctors there. Somehow that had given Bert the idea that I was the one who was keeping him locked up. He was insane, of course, though if you hadn't been around him much he could seem quite normal. He had a knife, and I shot him. The next morning I came to this house; I knew Elaine had spent most of the night at the hospital and would sleep late, but I told the housekeeper I had to talk to her about straightening up at the school. As I had expected, the housekeeper wouldn't wake her; but she let me wait again in Harry's study, and I put back the gun."

Elaine stood up, her violet eyes brimming with tears. "De Witte, I won't let you do this. You're a wonderful person— the best, the most unselfish man I've ever known. But I'm not going to let you destroy yourself. Lieutenant Sandoz, those are lies. De Witte is Harry's friend, his best friend, and now he's trying to save Harry, but it's not right."

Sandoz was up now, too, trying to get Elaine back into her chair. "Just let him tell his story, Mrs. Hollander. Hear him out." Between them I saw my father's face as if it were a photo in a frame; his mouth was open, but I don't think he was saying anything.

"Lieutenant," my mother said, *"I saw my husband with that box open!"*

23
How Blue Did the Job

ALL of a sudden it got so quiet in our living room you could hear yourself breathe.

Elaine dropped back into her chair and put her face in her hands. "I came into the study, and he was at the table. The box was open. He didn't see me. There. It's out. I said it."

"*Elaine!*" It was my father. "My God, Elaine!"

Blue said, "Yes, Elaine. My God." I'd never heard him use that tone before. Everybody looked at him, even her. "You saw your husband with Pandora's Box open, and you didn't ask why he had opened it? Why not? And by the way, what was in it?"

There were tears streaking my mother's perfect little face; I don't think she wanted to say anything, but after a minute she did. "Nothing. There was nothing in it when I saw it."

"You didn't see him put the German shell in it?"

"No, of course not. I wouldn't have gone through with the drawing."

"But you went through with it believing that the box was

182

empty? Thinking the whole thing would end in an excru-
ciating anticlimax?"

"I had to. There wasn't anything else to do."

Once I heard my father fire a man; it was the chauffeur
we had before Bill, and my father had told him to clear out
in just the tone he used now. What he said this time was,
"Lieutenant, I never opened that box."

"Mr. Hollander, I'm beginning to think you didn't."

Blue paid no attention to them. "There was everything
else to do, Elaine. All you would have had to do—if you'd
actually seen your husband with that box open, and the box
was empty—was suggest to him that you find some interesting antique to put in it as a prize. For a hundred dollars
you could have gotten some nineteenth-century books from
De Witte Sinclair. You could have used an old gun, or some
antique silver. Anything—anything, if you had really seen
it open as you say."

"Are you accusing me of having put the shell in that box?"

"Yes, I am," Blue told her. "I can prove it. I will prove
it."

Sandoz snorted. "First Mr. Hollander, then Sinclair, and
now Mrs. Hollander? Okay, let's hear it." He sounded
skeptical; but I was watching his eyes, and they told Jake
to get behind my mother. Jake did it, just a couple of steps
over.

Blue said, "Mr. Sinclair's confession was simply a trick,
as you certainly understand by now. He and I arranged it
over the telephone last night, and this morning he came to
my place and we rehearsed it."

Sandoz said, "He was running one hell of a risk."

Blue nodded. "He really is Mr. Hollander's best friend,
you see. Even rich and powerful men sometimes have one
or two real friends, though often they don't know it. We
took a few precautions, however; Mr. Sinclair can produce
three witnesses, including myself, who will swear that we
heard him express his intention to make a *false* confession

this morning. And it any event a polygraph test would have cleared him."

Sandoz grunted. "You claimed a minute ago that you could prove Mrs. Hollander made the bomb." He was watching her and pretending not to. "If you can, why'd you need Sinclair?"

"Because I'm trying to do something you police never seem to. I'm trying to anticipate the trial." Blue leaned back in his chair. It couldn't have been noon yet, but he looked tired. "The wisest thing for Mrs. Hollander to do would probably be to confess and throw herself upon the mercy of the court. That is what I would advise her to do if I were still an attorney, as I once was, and if I had somehow been chosen to represent her; but I don't believe she'll do it. Despite all that fragile beauty, she's a stubborn, not very shrewd fighter, and she's accustomed to getting what she wants."

Sandoz grunted again. "So?"

"To a great degree the success of her defense will depend on the support she receives from her husband, both in testimony and finance. Yesterday, when I went into Mr. Hollander's study, I noticed that a German eighty-eight-millimeter artillery shell was missing from his mantel; I won't bore you now by explaining how I knew that one had been there earlier. In conversation, I brought up the subject of artillery and waited for his reaction. There was none. It seemed clear he had no idea that the 'bomb' that exploded at the Fair had in fact been a shell. That hadn't been on the news, remember, and he had returned only an hour or two before from New York."

My father nodded. "You're right, I didn't know it then."

"When I talked to him," Blue continued, "he was eager that the murder of his brother should be avenged, which seemed quite natural. He was even more anxious, however, that the explosion at the Fair should not be investigated; since his wife had been deeply involved in the Fair and his daughter had been one of the casualties, that seemed un-

184

natural indeed. If he did not, as it appeared he did not, know that his shell had been used to build the bomb, it seemed probable that he was protecting someone else whom he assumed to be guilty; it was not difficult to guess who that was, or to see that he felt confident that the bombing and his brother's murder were unrelated."

Blue glanced at my father, then went back to Sandoz. "When you told him about the shell, he involuntarily glanced up at the mantel, and his shock was apparent. He knew at that moment, and with certainty, who had planted that bomb; but he did not accuse her. He loved his wife, and he must have known of her relations with Lief and believed she had given herself to him, and killed him, because of some hold he had over her. I needed to make her do or say something that would show her husband clearly not only that she had killed those people, but that she had planned her crime so he would be blamed."

My father said, "You did. Can you also tell me why she did it?"

"No," Blue said. "But she can, and perhaps eventually she will. All I can say now is that it appears to me that Lief was not her primary target—that worked out too neatly. I think she contrived to have an affair with the man who would open the box, in other words, and not that she contrived that the man with whom she had an affair would open it. And certainly her target was not originally Herbert Hollander the Third; his death bears the earmarks of a spur-of-the-moment decision. But until she said she had seen you with the box open, she might have argued, for example, that she had killed Lief because he was threatening to reveal their relationship to you unless she would run away with him. If she had done that, would you have helped her?"

"I suppose I would. I would have done whatever lay in my power, I think."

Elaine looked at him and saw that it was no good now, and looked away.

Molly's twangy voice surprised us. "I was wishin' a while ago I'd brought my gun to this, but I see it was the Good Lord's provision. I'd have shot Mr. Sinclair—or maybe not, 'cause a man that's been messed over by a bad woman has to be forgiven a lot. Miz Hollander, I didn't hate you like I ought to have when I heard about those letters of yours, 'cause Larry was just so handsome and good and I believed I knew how you'd felt. Now I know you didn't ever love him. You killed him just for bait, and I'll get you. I may have to wait till the law lets you go, but 'fore the world ends, you're mine."

Elaine couldn't meet her eyes, and everybody was quiet for a minute. It was my father who broke it. "Go on, Mr. Blue."

Blue leaned forward, looking from him to Molly, then over at Sandoz. "There were three plausible, but false, assumptions that tended to confuse things, I would say. The first may have impeded you more than it did me, Lieutenant. It was that the male voice that had threatened Larry over the telephone belonged to the person who contrived his death. Even when you decided that no vengeful veterans existed, I believe you thought those calls had been someone's effort to throw any investigation off track."

"And they weren't?"

"No, they weren't. Molly, do you want to explain now?"

Molly shook her head and looked at me. I said, "Larry made those calls himself. Molly says she was never completely sure, but I think she knew and just didn't let on. When she showed me her gun in the store—it was Larry's really, one they kept under the counter in case of a holdup— it was so I wouldn't guess she thought it was him. She says the voice told her some things it seemed like nobody but Larry would know. Were you onto him?"

Blue shook his head. "He came to me a month ago, brought by a mutual friend. I was interested in harassing calls, as I still am, so I poked around. By the time Larry was killed, I was considering the possibility that he had placed them himself, but I was far from sure. Now I see—or think I do—that he was tormented by guilt. If I'd exposed him, perhaps that would have provided punishment enough. There's no way of knowing."

"What'd he do?" I asked. When I saw how Molly was looking at me, I added, "I mean, I know it's none of my business . . ."

Blue said, "It is your business, actually. It's everyone's. I have no idea what Larry did, but I doubt that he did anything worse than many hundreds of others. There are no good wars, and Vietnam was a particularly bad one; many of its combatants wore civilian clothes, and much of the fighting took place in densely populated areas. If you desire speculation, mine would be that Larry believed that what he was doing was right, at first. And that by the time he'd changed his mind he'd been given, or was about to get, his commission. A month is a long time in war, and he may have gone on for months acting much as he had before, all the while becoming increasingly certain that he was morally a criminal. A protracted period during which a man acts against his conscience can produce severe psychic stress, though it is invisible at the time. Eventually, of course, he resigned that commission and left the service."

"You're telling us he brought back his own shell," my father said, "as I did." He looked old, I thought.

Sandoz cleared his throat. "You were talking about three wrong assumptions, and even if you were too polite to say I made them all, I'd like to know what the others were."

"I was led astray by the other two myself," Blue admitted. "One was that some sort of mechanism had to have been assembled to detonate the shell; that seemed to point to Lief and suicide, or to Mr. Hollander, who has an elaborate shop in the basement of this house and is reported to be a clever mechanic. It was a day and more after the explosion before it occurred to me that even before someone had put a bomb in it, Pandora's could have been no ordinary box. A long, long time ago, someone had taken the trouble to have that word, *Pandora,* lettered on its lid in gold leaf. Last night I escorted Holly home and helped her up the stairs, to the best of my ability. And as I was going out, it struck me that the collection of books on vaults and locks in Mr. Hollander's study might include references to such a box."

"I should have thought of that myself," Sandoz said. "Did it?"

My father said, "Yes, it does, and I would imagine from what Mr. Blue has said that he found at least one of them."

Sandoz looked at him. "You knew about it, then?"

"Certainly."

"Did you tell your wife what you knew?"

My father shook his head. "Why should I? The Pandoras were harmless, and as I saw it I'd only have been spoiling her fun." He paused, and I thought he was waiting for her to say something; she didn't, so he went on. "They belong to a class of gadgets called alarm boxes, and were made about a hundred years ago in fair numbers by an outfit called the Dependable Manufacturing Company. They came equipped with a good lock—by which I mean with a lock that was good by the standards of the period, before the introduction of pin tumblers—but they had a second line of defense, which is why we call them alarm boxes. In the Pandoras, it consisted of a spring-wound motor that rang a bell and fired a blank cartridge unless a secret catch on one side was pressed before the box was opened."

Blue said, "The people who built those boxes weren't out to create a murder weapon. The unrifled barrel that held the blank cartridge was not, as you might assume, directed toward the face of the unauthorized opener. It pointed toward the back of the box. The most common method of clearing what was a battlefield of unexploded shells is to detonate them by shooting them from a safe distance with a rifle. Mr. Hollander, who appears to have seen a good deal of action in World War II, may have mentioned that to his wife." Blue looked at Elaine. "Did he?"

Sandoz said, "So all she had to do was put a real bullet in the barrel."

"Yes, and position the shell so the bullet would strike it. No expert mechanic was required for either, of course. Holly here has a twenty-two rifle—I saw it in a corner of her bedroom—and everyone seems to have known about Mr. Hollander's PPK; a man who is often away and keeps a gun for protection generally tells his wife where to find it in any case. It's quite possible there are other guns in this house as well. Presumably there is one that uses ammunition that could be made to fit the Pandora's chamber. You were patient while I aired my speculations about Larry Lief. Do you want to hear a few more?"

"Shoot," Sandoz said. I don't think he was trying to be funny.

"I don't believe Mrs. Hollander was at all sure the shell would explode. If it had not, it would have served her purpose nearly as well. The world would have thought her husband had tried to kill her lover, and I imagine she would have persuaded her husband that her lover had arranged that it should."

"Hey!" I said. "Do you remember that I said the letter in the paper showed that the bomb did more than it was meant to?"

Blue nodded, and Sandoz asked him, "She wrote that?"

"I think so. If you haven't found the machine it was typed on—"

"We haven't."

"—and you've examined any that may be here, I'd suggest you look at those in the Chicago offices of the Hollander Safe and Lock Company, and particularly the one used by Mr. Hollander's secretary. On two occasions he told me he thought the bombing was the work of terrorists, although even the first time he must have suspected otherwise. No doubt he made the same remark to his wife by telephone from New York, and she—knowing by then of the calls the Liefs had received, which had been publicized by television news—wanted to make it look as though he was blowing smoke in the eyes of the police. Actually the letter struck me as having been written by a woman; thus it was a confirmation of the theory I had already formed."

"Before you get off onto that," I said, "what was the third wrong assumption?"

"That Pandora's box could only have been opened by someone skilled in picking locks."

Uncle Dee smiled. "Which I, by the way, am not." It was his real one, back home again.

"Eventually I did a little more research on Pandora's story—something I ought to have done much earlier. I told Holly one version shortly before the bomb went off. There is another, in which Pandora is given a box full of evils and told to guard it, but opens it out of curiosity. That one, of course, must have been what the Dependable Manufacturing Company had in mind, and its moral is that women are insatiably curious. I might mention in passing that I myself am more curious than any woman I have ever met.

"When I read the story, I realized how unlikely it was that Mrs. Hollander should have such a box, and offer it as a prize, without knowing what it contained. No doubt she could have had her husband open it in advance; but if she had, he would surely have guessed later that it was she who had arranged for his war souvenir to be in it and for the blank gun to be loaded. He did in any event, as we know, but that was certainly something she would have sought to avoid. She might have had the man she had made her lover, Larry Lief, open it; but if the shell failed to explode, or he survived the blast, or—as would have been quite possible—he had leaked the secret, she would again have been in great danger."

Sandoz said, "You're going to tell me she opened it herself with a hairpin."

Blue shook his head. "She opened it herself with the key. The conviction we all had that Pandora's box was locked, and, as it were, sealed, when she bought it rested upon her unsupported statement. Her statement was a lie. The box's alarm mechanism had been exhibited and explained to her before she purchased the box, and the key accompanied it. I doubt that you'll find it; once she had closed the box and relocked it, the key was merely a danger, and a key is an easy thing to dispose of."

Elaine said, "There wasn't any key!"

"Yes, there was," Blue told her. "Yesterday I located the shop where you bought the box, and had a conversation with its owner." He took one of those mini-cassette recorders out of the side pocket of his jacket. "Do you want to hear it?"

"No," Elaine said. She looked at us—my father, Blue and Sandoz and Uncle Dee, Molly and me. "I think this is the point at which I'm supposed to dash upstairs and blow out my brains with Holly's little rifle."

Behind her chair, Jake rumbled, "No you don't, lady."

"That's right. No, I don't. I'm going to get help, and we're going to fight this."

Hearing her I felt funny. It was the kind of thing I might have said myself.

24

How I Got My Job

THE next time I saw Blue I could walk. The Ford wagon that had been Mrs. Maas's was mine, and I had my stereo and clothes and all my junk in the back, with Sidi's saddle and some other tack I'd saved. The trees around Blue's place were already starting to turn when I lugged my portable up the porch steps; it'd been a dry summer.

Muddy came out to help me with my stuff just like he'd been expecting me; I suppose he thought I'd already spoken with Blue. In a minute I saw Blue in one of the front windows watching us, and went inside to talk to him. "I'm moving in," I said.

"So I see. May I ask why?"

"My father closed the house up and put it on the market. You know that?"

Blue nodded.

"This big place ought to have lots of bedrooms, and there's only the three of you living in it."

"We have guests occasionally; besides, some of the original bedrooms have been converted to other uses."

"No room for me?"

I was trying to look down, and I must have pulled it off, because Blue's voice got softer. "We'll make room for you, if we must. But what are you doing here?"

"My father set it up for me to stay with Les and her folks. I've still got a year before graduation, and he said he didn't want me to have to switch schools. He's got a townhouse down on the Gold Coast. That's in Chicago, next to the lake."

"I know where it is."

"Only Les's folks don't really go for having me around all that much, and living in the same house, Les and I don't hit it off like we used to. So I thought of you. I get an allowance—I could pay fifty a month, and I know you could use it. Besides, there's some questions I have to ask you."

Muddy came in then with my stereo and said, "How about the room in back?"

Blue shook his head. "The big turret. It's traditional."

So that's how I got to be a princess, captive in her tower. Don't ask me what Blue thinks he is; he's no giant, for sure. A dragon, maybe, or a warlock. If that's what he is, then I'm a warlock's secretary. I do his typing for him (he's only a two-finger typist, and he doesn't have a machine of his own anyhow), and when I answer the phone I say, "Aladdin Blue's office."

Only I'm getting a little ahead of the story. That evening we had a vegetarian dinner, the whole thing picked right out of Tick's garden, and I got my questions in. Muddy wanted to know about some letter Blue'd gotten, and Blue said that judging from the tone of it there wouldn't be any money in the job unless he could find some on the side. That gave me my opening. I said, "Do you remember that morning in our living room? You said the letter in the paper had been written by a woman. How did you know?"

"You have a fine memory." Blue looked thoughtful for a minute. There was some pretty good summer squash on his

plate—I happen to like squash—and he picked up a piece
with his fork and then set it down. "For one thing, there
was a great deal of underlining. Most people agree that
women have a penchant for that type of emphasis, although
you could probably find quite a few men who underline
more than the average woman. What seemed to me more
telling was the use, in a brief letter, of the words *bravely*
and *cheerfully*. Those are female words; men scarcely ever
employ them. I think that says something good about
women or something bad about men, though I'm not certain
what. It was only an indication, of course, not evidence."

"You said that was the second indication you had that
my . . . Elaine . . ." I drank a little coffee to get my voice
straightened out.

"Holly, are you sure you want to talk about this?"

"I have to. So tell me. What was the first one?"

"The rose you found in the bouquet in your hospital room,
of course."

"You said I had a memory. I'd nearly forgotten about
that, and anyway I don't see what it means."

"It meant that the police were wrong in thinking your
uncle had been shot when he arrived at the hospital. You
said it was a florist's rose, remember? And that he must have
persuaded the florist to insert it in your mother's bouquet.
That seemed very improbable to me. What appeared much
more plausible was that he had bought a single rose, which
would have cost only a couple of dollars, and brought it to
the hospital himself; or that he had gone into some other
room—one in which the patients were asleep—and taken
the rose from an arrangement there. Once he'd done that,
the natural place to put it would be the vase that already
held your mother's bouquet. But either explanation implied
that he had been not only in the hospital but in your room;
and your mother, we knew, had been in that room with you
for a good part of the night."

"So she'd seen him. Wasn't his name on the register? And why did she kill him, anyway?"

"No, he wasn't on the register. But then he would not have dared to register. To be admitted, he would have had to explain his relationship to you, and hospitals, especially, are alerted when a mental patient escapes. However, I doubt that a man who had succeeded in escaping from a mental institution would find it difficult to slip past a sleepy receptionist. Perhaps he was in your room when your mother arrived, though it is more likely that he came somewhat later. In any event, they left together and he died in the parking lot."

"She was carrying my father's gun around, then."

Blue nodded.

"Why?"

"I don't know. Possibly simply because she was frightened. If her love letters to Larry had not been found, she would have had to see to it that Larry's to her were, in order to provide a motive for your father. She may have been afraid of what Molly might do when they were made public. Or perhaps she had planned all along to kill someone with your father's gun. Perhaps she planned to kill him and make it appear a suicide, though I doubt that."

"I guess I still don't understand what she was after." I took another swallow of coffee and made a face.

"Freedom."

"Yeah, and money. For her I guess there wasn't any freedom without money. But what was she doing? Why Uncle Herbert?"

"Again—remember the day I talked to you in the hospital. You said you were rich, but later you called that a lie and said you merely came from a rich family. Even your second statement wasn't quite true, as wealth is measured in Barton Hills. Your father was the president of a medium-sized corporation. He was paid an excellent salary, but that salary was all he had. The real wealth belonged to your uncle; it was merely administered by your father."

"Sure, I knew that."

"If your father had died, your mother would have been left with his insurance and his house—ten times more money than most human beings ever see, but not enough to permit her to live as she wished to live."

"She could've killed Uncle Herbert, then killed my father."

"Possibly she could have, though murdering your uncle would have been difficult as long as he remained in Garden Meadow; but she was intelligent enough, I think, to see that if she were to kill them both she lacked the brilliance to escape conviction. Those murders would have directed a much less astute policeman than Lieutenant Sandoz to her. What actually happened was that your father received a letter which seemed to indicate that your uncle had not long to live. That event, I would guess, suggested a much more subtle plan.

"She had already purchased Pandora's Box and loaded it with two iron buggy weights—they were used to hitch the horse when there was no post or rail—so that Bill wouldn't think it empty. Servants talk, you know, and at that time she was very probably planning to put some interesting antique in the box, just as I suggested later."

"Those were the weights that Sandoz found under the sofa in the study?"

"Yes. She should have disposed of them before then, but at the time neither Sandoz nor I had any idea why they were there. Perhaps I should mention that it was Bill, whom they were meant to deceive, who directed me to the shop where she had bought the box. I telephoned him from the kitchen while you were sitting in my office."

"But when the letter came, she figured out how to use the box."

Blue nodded again. "She would kill in such a way that

196

your father would be blamed. While he was in prison, your uncle would, she thought, die of natural causes. Your father would inherit—nothing in the law bars a prisoner from claiming an inheritance, provided it does not come to him by his crime. She, his wife, would control that money for so long as he remained imprisoned, probably for the remainder of his life."

"Only when he figured out that he was going to die, Uncle Herbert went over the fence."

Muddy said, "So would I, if I knew I was about to croak—I mean if I was locked up someplace. Al, how about a couple more of these thin-sliced tomatoes?"

I held out my plate. "I'd like some more, Muddy."

"Swell. Everything's organically grown and good as hell for you."

"You think she just decided to hurry things up?"

"I doubt it," Blue said. "Perhaps she anticipated the sort of situation Lieutenant Sandoz envisioned—your uncle's starting a legal fight to remain free. Or perhaps she let something slip there in your hospital room that indicated she had planted the bomb, and shot your uncle to silence him. My best guess is that he knew how the Pandora boxes worked—he had been raised to take over the family business, remember—and he said enough in your hospital room to frighten her. Certainly he had been to the site of the explosion, since he must have picked up your rose there. No doubt he had talked to people who described the drawing, but we'll never know unless she tells us."

Muddy said, "Tomorrow I'm gonna stew some with bread crumbs and green peppers."

That about winds it up; you don't have to read this last part if you don't want to. Bullets from the gun in my father's desk matched the bullet they took out of Uncle Herbert, and the police found a nurse's aide who'd seen him and Elaine leaving together, so that was the one they tried her on. About once a month I hitch downstate to visit her, but I haven't used any of the stuff she's told me in the visiting room when I put together this book, because it's different almost every time. My father still has his place on the Gold Coast, only now there's a woman named Marcie living with him; she's maybe five years older than I am. I haven't seen him for a couple of months, but yesterday I got him a birthday card at Ozco's, and when I send this off to the first publisher on my list I'm going to mail his card to him. Maybe it'll remind him my own birthday's coming up pretty quick now. You never know.